Evie, the Star Princess

Phil Rosenberg

iUniverse books may be ordered through booksellers or by contacting:

iUniverse
1663 Liberty Drive
Bloomington, IN 47403
www.iuniverse.com
1-800-Authors (1-800-288-4677)

Because of the dynamic nature of the Internet, any web addresses or links contained in this book may have changed since publication and may no longer be valid. The views expressed in this work are solely those of the author and do not necessarily reflect the views of the publisher, and the publisher hereby disclaims any responsibility for them.

Any people depicted in stock imagery provided by Getty Images are models, and such images are being used for illustrative purposes only.
Certain stock imagery © Getty Images.

ISBN: 978-1-5320-4442-7 (sc)
ISBN: 978-1-5320-4443-4 (e)

Library of Congress Control Number: 2018903414

Print information available on the last page.

iUniverse rev. date: 03/27/2018

To Evie, the granddaughter, the kind, the cute, the funny, the beautiful. She wants to do the right thing for others. What a difference she will make in the world!

CONTENTS

ACKNOWLEDGMENTS

The main character in this fictional storybook found her way into my brain and into my heart. She breached all my defenses, which almost always work to keep that kind of brain invasion from happening. Evie took over my mind and told me very clearly that she would not leave until her story unfolded in the pages of this book. Her voice helped drive me toward being able to share her adventures, challenges, and joys with you.

However, it took a skilled and dedicated surgical team to help me extract the character successfully when the book was finished. My team—or, as Evie and her grandpa would say, my "army"—of supporters clearly begins with my guiding star, my amazing and beautiful wife of nearly five decades, Charlotte. Thank you for your support, editing, ideas, and encouragement.

I acknowledge and thank the amazing HR daughter Elyse Rosenberg, who has not only followed in my public service career footsteps but already hiked higher and farther than I have traveled. The people of Portland, Oregon, are incredibly lucky to have her in their city government!

Fantastic doctor and daughter Rachel Brown is not only a lead character in the book but also a highly skilled, caring family practice physician and mother. Together, these two daughters have always made me proud, have never disappointed me, and have always encouraged me in the writing of *Evie and the Magic Telescope*; *Evie, the Star Princess*; *Don't Walk by Something Wrong!* and more than five hundred articles published nationally over the years.

That wonderful and always appreciated level of support comes also from great son-in-law Matt Kramer, Elyse's husband, and Tim Harris, Rachel's significant other.

Of course, the gorgeous granddaughter and model for the main character in this and a prior book is Evie herself! I could not ask for a smarter, funnier, and more loving granddaughter. My job as Grandpa is not only to provide hugs and cuddles but also to do everything I can do to ensure that Evie's future is bright and that the world comes to know how much better off it is because she is part of it.

Evie's dad, Toby, is very much a part of the equation that makes her a very special person, and I thank him every day for serving so well in that critical role.

Many people were asked to read the manuscript and help me with their commentary and critique. I thank them all—you know who you are! I send a special thank-you to astronomers Ernie Rossi, Al Broxton, and Stu Anderson for loaning me their sympathetic and critical minds and eyeballs in reviewing this book. The same is true of Skip and Marlene Honigstein, John and Michele Uss, Gina Rossi, Christine Broxton, and Joan Anderson—friends whose good counsel I appreciate greatly. They helped keep *Evie, the Star Princess* fun to write and fun to read (I hope!).

Finally, and certainly worth mentioning, are two of my closest friends and critics of a different species. They were often on the floor next to me as I wrote much of this book. They frequently reminded me that there are many more important things than finishing a book, including letting them out to go for a romp in the meadows (and a chance to pee) and taking time out to practice rolling over, fetching the newspapers, and trying to say "I love you" in canine language.

Taken altogether, this is a powerful team to have in your corner when you are doing something wonderful—or, frankly, when any other circumstances remind you of the great value of friends and family members.

PROLOGUE

She was a shy little girl who was uncertain about her future. Evie was more comfortable with adults than with children her age, and she didn't have many friends. She would be the one who sat near the back of her elementary school classroom and didn't often raise her hand. She could be overwhelmed by the pressure put on her by other students, in particular a classroom bully who made others sad and afraid. Her classmates were unsure of what to do.

All of that changed for Evie when she spent part of the summer at Grandpa and Grammie's farm far out in the country. In a mysterious white building with a roof that looked like a big cereal bowl turned upside down, Evie was introduced to a very special new friend, a friend full of magic waiting to be shared with Evie.

Soon after she arrived at the farm, on a clear night when the stars were bright, she and Grandpa slowly walked toward this unusual building. It was out in the pasture, away from other buildings and any lights.

At the building's gleaming doorway, a shiny golden key was set inside a lock. Following Grandpa's instructions, she turned the key. At once, mysterious and amazing things began to happen. Part of the building moved out of the way, and Evie found herself looking up in wonder as Grandpa introduced her to Angelina, the magic telescope.

That was the beginning of Evie's adventure! The shy young girl found her passion in the weeks she spent with Angelina. Together they explored the night sky. Evie and the magic telescope visited many wonders deep in the night sky. With help from Grandpa and Angelina, she learned about these objects. She learned to photograph them, and she studied them using the many books in Grandpa's library. They spent hours together in the big white observatory!

Her wondrous adventures with Angelina the magic telescope changed Evie very much. She returned home and returned to school at the end of the summer as a person who had a clear vision of her future life. Angelina was indeed a magic telescope. She had transformed the shy and worried Evie into a confident girl full of knowledge and talent. Evie was going to be an explorer of the sky and an inspiration to others!

Join Evie as she settles back into the classroom. She can't wait for the next set of adventures to begin. Little does she know what incredible adventures those will be!

CHAPTER 1

EVIE THE EXCHANGE SISTER

After her summer adventures with Angelina the magic telescope, the next school year seemed to fly by for Evie. She practiced her music and studied her astronomy books every day. When the night sky was clear, and the stars were bright, Evie was often outside with her telescope, computer, and camera. She would practice setting up equipment, taking photographs, and exploring the beauty of the night. She also learned other skills, including a lot about medicine, first aid, and biology, from her mother. Dr. Rachel knew very well how important education was and how important it was to be a person with many different skills. After all, Dr. Rachel had enjoyed her own college years, and even the very hard medical school years, because she could make friends easily and have fun learning with people from many different places in the world.

When Dr. Rachel was growing up, her dad (Evie's grandpa) and her mom (Evie's grammie) invited six exchange students, one after the other, from Europe and Japan to live with the family as brothers and sisters for six months to a year. Becoming an exchange student meant showing people respect, confidence, the ability to speak another language, curiosity, and a sense of humor. Rachel learned the importance of these traits as she got to know each of her exchange student brothers and sisters.

Monika from Germany showed Rachel how important it was to laugh and to play music. Monika always had a flute in her backpack. She also helped the future Dr. Rachel understand how important it was to work hard at school and do homework on time.

Rachel learned the importance of spending time with the family and discussing world affairs, science, art, history, and much more every night. Grammie, Grandpa, and Rachel would stop watching television or staring at a computer screen and spend time discussing the news of the world whenever they had dinner together. They discussed what had happened at school that day; what had happened at the farm; and what everybody hoped would happen in the coming days, months, and years.

From Kazumi, her Japanese exchange student sister, Rachel learned about appreciating the beauty of nature. She learned about trust and how people sometimes struggle to communicate. She learned that those struggles, especially involving different cultures, great distances, and different languages, could be overcome by a warm smile, a sense of humor, and a desire to learn. Rachel learned the importance of finding people who could teach her things about life.

Later, in high school, Rachel herself became an exchange student and spent time in a small village in Germany. She told Evie all about her adventures there, including family bike rides to the village with a special stop at the village ice cream shop. She described her time spent in school, where everyone spoke German and was eager to help Rachel learn quickly. They all said Rachel was a wonderful ambassador for her family, for her country, and for people in general.

It was not a surprise to Mom when Evie asked whether they too could have an exchange student live with them, just as Grammie and Grandpa did when Rachel was young. Mom smiled at Evie and told her that exchange students are very special. "They are smart, educated, brave, and respectful," she told Evie. "They would not only love to spend time in America, but they would be great friends and role models." She told Evie that she would be very happy to be the host mom for an exchange student in the future.

Knowing that she would have an exchange brother or sister in the next school year helped Evie work even harder at learning about other countries, as well as geography, current events, history, science, and music. While working through an organization called Youth for Understanding, which helped match students with host parents, Evie and her mom chose Rita Gallin, a high school senior from Chile, to spend one semester with them. Rita played the piano very well, and she loved to explore new places and meet new people.

It was not difficult for Evie to choose which language she would study in school in addition to English; she chose Spanish. Having a Spanish-speaking exchange sister made the choice easier. So did the fact that several of her classmates spoke Spanish and had family members who'd come to the United States to work hard for a better life. She had often played with these friends and did homework with them at their houses. She enjoyed listening to the music they loved, eating the foods they ate, and participating in their favorite hobbies. Some liked painting and jewelry making—skills they'd brought with them when they came to America years earlier. Like the exchange students who Mom talked about, these friends were particularly brave in coming to a new country. Evie admired how quickly they were learning English and how hard they worked. She helped them with their homework sometimes, and in turn, they helped her with her Spanish skills and shared stories about their own travels and former countries. That helped Evie grow and learn.

Together, Evie and Rita often went shopping, played duets on the violin and piano, and talked endlessly about the hopes each one had for a wonderful, fun life. "It will be very hard to say goodbye to you at the end of semester, Rita. You have become a very wonderful friend," Evie said with a tear in her eye. Evie had found an older sister, and Mom had found a second daughter! Rita now had an American family, as well as her family in Chile. Promises were made that the two families would meet someday, perhaps in Chile, and that Evie and Rita would write to each other regularly and use video chats often. Rita was studying to be a businesswoman, perhaps even to take over her father's large construction company when he retired. Rita admired Evie's passion and learned a large amount about the wonders of deep space objects during her time with Evie and her mom.

CHAPTER 2

WHEN YOU ARE AFRAID ...

Even as a very young child, Evie already understood that everyone had worries and fears. Her mom talked with her about how worried some of her patients were about their futures when she had to give them bad news about a medical problem they faced. "No one, not an adult or a child, is immune from feeling uncertain about things from time to time," Mom told her.

Evie had also learned from role models that when she was afraid or worried, knowing that she had friends and family members to help her made a very big difference. In fact, Evie already knew that being with other people was powerful treatment against fear. Phoning her friends or visiting with them when she felt sad was a big help. She could see how important it was to have many friends. All she had to do was to watch school athletic teams come together and support each other. The same was true of musical groups like orchestras and bands, and even local clubs and social groups. She saw the power of friends helping friends when the mother of one of her friends passed away after a serious illness. Many people came to help her friend. Simply having people who cared around made a very big difference.

Evie's mom and dad had divorced when she was very young. However, Evie had absolutely no doubt that she was loved very much by both of them. She would spend time with each of them. "I'm a lucky girl," she would say. "I have two rooms of my own, two pets to play with in two different places, and neighbors and friends at both neighborhoods."

Evie's mom spent a lot of time in her busy medical career, and Evie's dad was very fortunate to be able to do a lot of his work from home. That meant that he could be there regularly when Evie came home from school, and he helped with homework and with meals. It meant that they had time to talk to each other and share their feelings.

He had a special career involving animals in faraway Africa. He had met a famous safari guide, and Evie would also meet him soon enough. Dad had told her all about the several safaris he had been on with his safari guide friend. Evie listened intensely when he told her about the close encounters he had with amazing animals that could be found all over the many game parks in South Africa. Dad had not only enjoyed watching the animals, but he'd enjoyed the safari guests from all over the world. All the guests agreed that their safari experiences would be lifelong memories.

One night, Evie's dad told her about a long conversation he and his new safari guide friend had. By the time that conversation ended, they had formed a business partnership. Dad became his American safari representative. Evie was very proud that Dad had helped thousands of people enjoy the spirit and adventure of African safaris. Evie knew that someday he would take her to Africa and share that wonder directly with her.

Evie had loving parents, and she knew that she could turn to each of them when she needed help or hugs. She knew that they would never abandon her when she needed their help. Grandpa said to her, "Evie, your parents are the most important members of your army." Now, besides her parents and Grandpa and Grammie, she also had an exchange sister in faraway Chile. Rita might be thousands of miles away in person, but she was as close as a phone call or computer clicks whenever Evie wanted to chat.

CHAPTER 3

EVIE'S FEAR OF PUBLIC SPEAKING

Time with Rita certainly improved Evie's Spanish skills, but she also learned another lesson that would help her throughout her years of schooling. In fact, this lesson shaped her career and her life.

Evie had gained great confidence by getting to know Angelina, the magic telescope. She was no longer the shy little girl who was reluctant to raise her hand in class and had few friends. However, there was a serious challenge that she needed to overcome in order to be truly happy and successful. Although she was no longer shy with her friends, Evie was very nervous and reluctant to speak to groups of people. She knew that learning to overcome this fear of public speaking was just as important for her future as learning the latest information about astronomy. What would it take for her to conquer this fear?

Three things emerged in this struggle that helped Evie tremendously. The first was wise advice she got from Grandpa. He told her that the fear of public speaking was not something she alone was facing. It was one of the greatest fears that any person felt. Evie knew that Grandpa's advice was based on many years of giving hundreds of lectures, speeches, and seminars.

She said, "Grandpa, were you ever afraid to stand up in front of an audience and speak, especially without any notes? If you were afraid, what did you do to overcome your fear?" She was very afraid of public speaking, and she needed and wanted help to overcome the fear.

Grandpa said to Evie, "I was often afraid and nervous, especially when I first started my career. However, a friend of mine told me about a technique he had used very successfully for a very long time. It was called directed imaging. Evie, try very hard to imagine that you weren't really standing in front of a large group of people with a microphone and lights glaring in your eyes! Whenever you speak to a group, imagine that this group is really just a small number of your best friends sitting in your house and enjoying each other's company and perhaps dessert. The thought of chocolate ice cream with your best friends can go a long way to help you become a powerful speaker."

Evie remembered laughing at this advice about directed imaging and chocolate. Later, she came to see that Grandpa was right! "You can overcome your fears if you turn them into more familiar surroundings in your mind," she thought.

A few days later, Grandpa told her about another powerful tool to overcome her fear of public speaking. "Find role models," he told her. He explained that role models were people she met or observed whose behavior and performance at school, in the community, or at home helped her learn. Grandpa said to Evie, "Your exchange sister, Rita, set a very good example. Even though English was not her native language, she had learned to speak with confidence and humor to other people and groups of people." Rita had told Evie that she too was afraid to speak in public or to speak with important people she met, such as her father's business associates, school teachers, and school administrators. Yet she did it! She learned to look them in the eyes, smile, and shake their hands with confidence when she met them. She would tell them her name and repeat theirs. She would say, "Hello, Mrs. Jones. My name is Rita Gallin." Repeating their name helped her remember them. It also made them feel more comfortable with Rita. She told them that it was a pleasure to meet them and that she looked forward to speaking with them. Even if she seemed confident on the outside, Rita told Evie that at first, it was difficult to really feel that way.

Over time, however, it became second nature to Rita to be more outgoing and confident about being in public. She became so good at meeting people that her dad would often ask her to go over to someone whose name he had forgotten and introduce herself. That way he could hear the person say the name! That advice helped Evie remember how, when growing up, she'd met friends of her mom's and dad's and felt comfortable being with adult friends. She would remember Rita's advice and behavior and apply those lessons when she spoke to groups. She looked forward to someday meeting Rita's dad and behaving just the way Rita did with him years earlier. That would no doubt make him smile!

Rita's story about her own fears also made Evie think about another important piece of advice from Grandpa: "Create your own army." Rita was part of Evie's army for sure! Her help made a big difference for Evie—and just when she needed it! Grammie also gave her some important advice. "Remember to take a deep breath and let the air out slowly before you start to speak! Imagine that when you breathe out you are sending away your fears."

Evie learned from her mom, her exchange sister, Grammie, and role models like her astronomy mentor, university professor Dr. Charles Chandler, that the lessons she learned were not going to help her very much without huge amounts of practice. The more she spoke in public, and the more she raised her hand in class to ask or answer questions, the more her skill would improve, and the less fear she would have. She thought to herself that this was just like learning to play the violin: practicing important skills was a key tool to learn.

By using these tools Evie, became a confident speaker with people she knew. She also became adept at speaking in front of large groups of people without having a script or rehearsing. She had learned to overcome her fear, especially if the subject was something like astronomy—a subject about which she was passionate and happy to speak to others.

As her fear of public speaking faded away, Evie felt ready for new adventures in a new school year, her first year as a confident explorer of the sky who knew what she wanted to make of herself.

CHAPTER 4

THE COLLEGE OBSERVATORY FIELD TRIP

It had been a couple of months since the school year began again. Evie's sixth-grade classmates and the teacher remembered the promise made at the end of the last school year about a field trip to the observatory. The teacher shared ideas and plans with Evie, and in turn, Evie got advice from Dr. Chandler and offered him her own ideas about what could happen. Plans were finally set for the trip in the early winter.

Evie's teacher asked her to write a letter to the parents to get permission for their children to be part of the trip. Evie was careful to write a short letter about why the trip would be fun and full of learning. She asked for parents to volunteer to help with the trip because there were nearly thirty students in her class. Her letter was written by hand by each student and sent home to discuss with parents.

The next day, parent permission slips began arriving. Within a week, every student would be allowed to go, and ten parents volunteered to come along. Everyone thought the trip was a wonderful idea. Parents were just as curious as their children about what might be inside the big silver dome of the observatory. No one in the class had ever visited before.

Dr. Chandler asked Evie to meet with him to plan the details of the visit. Evie, her mom and dad, and the teacher went to the observatory, and they spent two hours with Dr. Chandler. By the time the meeting was over, the whole visit had been planned. Parent volunteers would make sure that all the children got to the observatory by six o'clock on the evening of the trip. The university would take care of dinner for the students and parents. Evie was excited to know that students in the university program who were learning to be chefs would be making the dinner and a special pastry dessert. Dinner would be held outside as long as the weather was good. In fact, it would be held right outside of the observatory building just as the sun was setting. By the time dinner was over, the first stars would be appearing in the twilight.

Evie volunteered to be in charge of welcoming her classmates and making sure that everyone enjoyed dinner. All of the people who did the cooking and the cleanup would be thanked after the meal. Evie would then introduce her teacher to everyone, and the teacher would introduce Dr. Chandler. He would describe the beauty of the sky and talk to the students about what they might be seeing that night in the heavens.

Dr. Chandler asked Evie about her favorite constellations and other objects in the sky during the early winter. Evie answered with confidence because she had thought a lot about it. She said, "My favorite constellation out of all eighty-eight of them is Orion, the hunter!"

"Why Orion?" asked the teacher.

Evie answered that there was a wonderful myth about Orion, and she told the story: "Orion was a great hunter, and he had with him two hunting dogs, Canis Majoris (the Great Dog) and Canis Minor (the Little Dog). He fell in love with the Seven Sisters (the Pleiades), but he couldn't get to them without fighting a giant, fierce bull named Taurus. The ancient gods put all of these characters of the myth into the sky so that people could know the story and remember it forever and ever."

Everyone agreed that the way Evie told the story made it exciting and made people want to pay careful attention. She could make the listeners want to learn more. Evie would be asked to tell the story when her classmates visited. Then it would be Dr. Chandler's turn.

Dr. Chandler said that he would like everyone to know about some of the amazing objects that are in these constellations. For instance, he would tell everyone about the Great Nebula. It could be found in what looks like a sword below the three stars of Orion's belt. He would tell about the "nursery" inside the nebula, where new stars were being born, and he would explain how that was happening.

Dr. Chandler wanted to show the students and parents what happened when some stars died. He would bring this part of the star's story to life by telling everyone about the Crab Nebula. This beautiful cloud of gases was created when a star exploded in a huge supernova blast. He would also describe the beauty of the Pleiades star cluster, the Seven Sisters. The constellations the students would see contained different types of stars. The giant telescope would show everyone bright, giant blue, red, and white stars. He would show everyone the brightest star in the night sky, Sirius, the Dog Star, in the Great Dog constellation. It would be a wonderful evening, and everyone would leave by ten o'clock at night.

Evie's teacher asked what would happen if everything was cloudy or rainy. "That is a very good question," Dr. Chandler said. "Astronomers always worry about the night sky cooperating when they have guests. Next door to the observatory is the planetarium. If it should rain, all of the students will go to the planetarium and see a program about the very stars and constellations I have just described. But don't worry about that. Evie and I have decided that the night will be clear and the temperature just right for everyone to have a wonderful time in the observatory!"

Finally, Dr. Chandler said all the students would be allowed to come into the observatory to learn how it worked. They would watch as the great dome turned and the huge shutter in the observatory dome opened up, so that the university telescope could be moved and pointed at the wonders he had just described. Every student would get to look through the huge telescope, aided by some of the students working on advanced degrees under the direction of Dr. Chandler. Several other telescopes would be set up, and some of them would have cameras attached.

It was clear that everybody in the meeting was very excited about what was to come. Dr. Chandler ended the meeting by saying, "Evie, thank you very much for making this class trip possible. I look forward to you being my assistant, helping me explain things to your classmates, and even answering some of their questions. In fact, I would love it if I could call on you several times during the class trip to explain things."

Evie was very excited indeed and gave Dr. Chandler a smile and a big hug.

CHAPTER 5

THE FIELD TRIP DAY IS HERE

Finally, the day of the field trip was at hand. For the past two weeks, everyone in class had science homework to do each night. They were asked by their teacher to read about the stars in their science books and at the library. They were asked to read about Orion the hunter in particular. They each got a star chart and instructions from Evie about how to use it. In their own backyards after dark, they could then use the star chart to learn about the stars. They had many questions, but it was easy to see how excited they were. On two of these nights, friends of Evie invited her to come to their houses. Evie talked with them and their parents about how to use the star chart. Evie was happy and excited to be a helper as her friends learned and prepared for the field trip.

The afternoon of the field trip, Evie and her mom got to the university early and saw how Dr. Chandler's students had set up the dinner tables, as well as how the controls for the big observatory dome worked. Dr. Chandler showed Evie different handouts that he had prepared to give to her classmates. Imagine Evie's surprise to find that photos of the Great Nebula in the constellation of Orion and the Crab Nebula in the constellation of Taurus, taken the year before with Grandpa, were included in Dr. Chandler's handouts! Dr. Chandler asked her if she knew about some of the objects they might see, like the Crab Nebula and the nursery of the stars in the Great Nebula. He smiled with pride as he heard Evie explain very clearly how the nebula came to be and how new stars would emerge from the Great Nebula's "nursery." Clearly, her time at Grandpa's observatory was well spent, as was the time she devoted to reading her astronomy books!

The parents and students arrived on time. Being on time was something their teacher stressed as very important; it was a sign of respect for other people. The dinner began promptly with wonderful food and a great dessert served by university students.

"Let us all thank the student helpers," Evie said. At that, her classmates applauded loudly, and so did the parents. Evie invited the food service students to join in for the program after dinner. It was a surprise for them, but one that she had discussed earlier with Dr. Chandler, who agreed that it would be a great idea.

The night was beautiful. Temperatures were cool but not too cold. Everyone was comfortable. The sky was clear, and the stars of the winter night shone brightly.

Evie spoke with excitement, knowledge, humor, and passion. "We are here tonight thanks to Dr. Charles Chandler and the university. We are here tonight thanks to our parents and the students from the university who are helping us. We are also here tonight thanks to Orion the hunter, the Seven Sisters, the strong hunting dogs, and even the fierce bull named Taurus. I want to tell you their stories."

For the next fifteen minutes, Evie told the stories of these and other constellations, and she pointed them out in the sky to her fellow students outside of the observatory.

She also told them stories about other constellations that were not visible at the time. In particular, she told them of the adventures of the great hero Perseus, who fell in love with the beautiful princess Andromeda. Andromeda's mother, Queen Cassiopeia, had insulted the gods, and a great monster was sent to kill Andromeda as punishment. Brave Perseus rescued her. The gods placed the princess, the queen, and the hero in the sky as constellations so that their story would never be forgotten.

She told them that all eighty-eight constellations are full of wonders that anyone can see by becoming an explorer of the sky. She told her classmates about how Dr. Chandler had many more surprises for them that night. She hoped they would ask questions. "I hope that after tonight, you will all go home and imagine how you could explore the sky's wonders, even from your own backyard with your parents! I hope that in school the next day, every one of you will come ready to learn more and take up a new hobby."

Dr. Chandler showed them around the observatory. He asked if one of the students would like to come forward and press the button he pointed at. This one would move the great shutter in the dome out of the way so that the telescope could see the evening sky. They all raised their hands and wanted to be able to do that. Dr. Chandler picked one from the class. That student got to push the button while everyone watched part of the mighty dome open.

Again a student was chosen to push a button. This time, the whole dome turned so that the shutter opening pointed to Orion. Every student's eyes were wide open as the huge dome turned, making sounds that could only come from a great machine with powerful motors. The same sense of wonder present on the faces of the students was also clearly visible on the excited faces of their parents.

The big telescope itself was already set up to point to the Great Nebula in the constellation of Orion. Dr. Chandler explained to the students what they would be seeing, especially the area of the nebula where new stars were forming. Each student got to look at the nebula through the telescope with the help of Dr. Chandler's students.

Phrases like "Wow!" "That's so beautiful!" and "Amazing!" echoed inside the dome. Several students said nothing; they later said they didn't know what to say because it was so incredible. They had never seen anything like that before. After everyone got to look through the huge telescope, Dr. Chandler attached a "live view" camera to it. That way the whole class could watch at the same time on the big television screens and see what the telescope was aimed at.

He asked for another volunteer, and all hands were raised again. Another student was selected to push a button, which moved the huge observatory dome again. The dome slowly turned, and everyone was breathless as they watched. Finally, the dome stopped, and another part of the sky was visible. Yet another student was chosen to push the buttons that moved the great telescope itself. It slowly turned as every student stared at it in amazement. Many looked at their parents and smiled. Some held their parents' hands tightly. The telescope stopped, and everyone looked at one of the most beautiful star clusters in the entire sky, the Pleiades (the Seven Sisters).

Dr. Chandler described the stars in that cluster. All eyes were glued to the TV screens. After a while, more student volunteers got to move the dome and then the telescope itself to the constellation Taurus to see the Crab Nebula. This was a huge cloud of gases created when the life of a star ended in a giant explosion. Astronomers in China over one thousand years ago got to see this giant explosion with their naked eyes. After all, they lived at a time when there were no electric lights, and cities were not very crowded. There were also far fewer people and much less air pollution, and so the skies were much darker.

The four-hour visit to the university observatory seemed to end more quickly than anyone wanted. Evie's friends had seen incredible wonders in the sky and even got to see the giant planet Jupiter. They got handouts from Dr. Chandler that included some of Evie's photos. They were also given free passes for themselves and another person to come to a planetarium show about the winter holidays.

Just before the program ended, Dr. Chandler invited Evie to come to the front of the room. He presented her with an official certificate from the university that named her as a friend of the observatory and an explorer of the sky. Everyone applauded.

Evie was surprised and felt very humble. She thanked Dr. Chandler, her teacher, and her mom. "It was very nice of you, Dr. Chandler, to host our class trip and to make my friends, our teacher, and the parents here feel so welcome. Thank you for the certificate, but thank you even more for being someone I look up to as I learn more about astronomy."

Then Dr. Chandler himself received a certificate from Evie's school naming him an honorary sixth grade teacher! Everyone left happy and chattering with each other and their parents about the wonders they had seen and how they wanted to learn more.

CHAPTER 6

A SPECIAL PHONE CALL

Months had passed since the class field trip. Evie's mom got a call from Dr. Chandler. He asked if he could meet again with her and Evie to talk about some ideas he had. Mom invited him to dinner a couple of days later and promised him a homemade apple pie. Evie always looked forward to the chance to spend some time with Dr. Chandler, and now he was coming to dinner again.

Ever since the class trip, Evie had become a regular observatory volunteer, fitting the time in between school, music lessons, and her Spanish lessons. She liked to spend at least a few hours once a week after school, and sometimes after dinner, at the observatory or the planetarium. Evie knew that her mom was very happy to go with her; Dr. Rachel sometimes brought along her medical journals and papers to read while Evie helped the students and staff members with their work. Evie would help them organize the planetarium shows and was even allowed to learn how the large planetarium projection system worked. Her mom had told her often that her kindness to the students, her knowledge of astronomy, and her sense of humor made her very proud.

The digital planetarium projector was amazing. Under the dark dome of the planetarium, when the lights dimmed, the person who operated the projector could make tens of thousands of stars, constellations, galaxies, nebulae, or planets appear on the dome. Movements of objects in the sky could be demonstrated. The sky could be shown as it was on any date in the past or future. The person who got to run the projection system became known as the sky pilot. Usually astronomy graduate students got to do the work. "I love driving the sky," Evie would tell her friends. "Maybe someday I will learn to drive a car!

However, Evie was so diligent in volunteering regularly and always being on time that she got special permission to spend time with some of the students and staff, learning how to use the equipment. Everyone, even the busy professional astronomers, liked getting to spend some time with Evie. Her sense of humor and curiosity made her fun to be around. They found her knowledge of astronomy to be very impressive for someone in middle school.

The more she learned, the more questions came to her mind. The more she learned, the more she wanted to learn. Her questions became more complicated, often causing her friends at the observatory to answer by saying, "I don't know. What do you think?" On the way home from the observatory, she would talk with her mom about what she did, the questions she'd asked, and how they were answered.

Evie had a particularly strong interest in the beautiful planet Saturn. Perhaps that was because it was the first object Evie got to see through Grandpa's big telescope. Saturn was so beautiful, and every time Evie looked at it, she felt like she had just visited a close friend.

And so it was that Evie couldn't get enough information about amazing Saturn. She read astronomy books and journals, talked to faculty and graduate students, and spent all the time she could in the observatory. Time using the big telescopes at the university was hard to come by; students had to sign up in advance for observing time for their own research projects. Time was also reserved for public visitor use. However, because everybody knew Evie and enjoyed her company, and because Dr. Chandler trusted her, she was also allowed to sign up for telescope time. Sometimes Mom would join her in the observatory, and sometimes other astronomers would also be there.

Evie created a list of observatory directors and wrote letters to them. She explained her interest in astronomy and her work as a volunteer. She learned what their names were and addressed each letter to them personally.

Dear Director Smith,

My name is Evie Brown. I am a middle school student, but my friends and mentors, such as Dr. Charles Chandler at the university, have told me that I am already an advanced student of astronomy. I am also a dedicated and regular volunteer at the observatory and at the planetarium. I am passionate about becoming an explorer of the sky.

I am writing to you with the hope that I might visit during the summer and see firsthand your work on the planet Saturn and the wonderful instruments available to you.

Thank you for considering my request. Please let me know when you think we might work out a time to visit.

Very sincerely yours,

Evie Brown
Explorer

Several directors wrote back to her. They invited her to visit and spend some time seeing how they did their research. One of those was the director of the Kitt Peak National Observatory in Arizona. The planet Saturn was one of the areas of great interest there. Some of the observatory staff members were specialists in Saturn, which made Evie all the more interested in visiting Kitt Peak. On the day set for dinner with Dr. Chandler, Evie wanted to ask him if he had ever visited Kitt Peak Observatory. She did not have to wait long because the doorbell rang, and it was time for dinner.

CHAPTER 7

EVIE RECEIVES AN OFFER

Mom had also invited the next-door neighbors to come to dinner. They were very good friends who had frequently watched Evie when Mom was called out suddenly to help someone who had become seriously ill. The neighbors loved Evie and enjoyed her excitement whenever the sky was mentioned.

Dinner was wonderful, especially the apple pie, which Evie had helped make. There was lots of chatter and laughing along with the sounds of enjoyable eating. Dr. Chandler brought with him another astronomy book to loan Evie. During dinner, he thanked her again for making the class trip possible. She said that she was the one to say thanks because the trip meant so much to everyone. She said to Dr. Chandler, "Everyone at school spent the whole next day talking about everything they saw in the big observatory. It was hard to focus on the rest of the subjects we had to study that day." She told Dr. Chandler that several students had asked her to come to their houses so that they could go out to the backyard and learn more about astronomy. Many students wanted to have telescopes of their own. She said their parents wanted to join in, and her school would form an astronomy club. She hoped that Dr. Chandler might be willing to help with that project.

He said, "Evie, that is very much what I have in mind to talk to you about. What I want to discuss with your mother and you wouldn't involve only the students in your class or in your school. It would go very much further than that!" After dinner, Dr. Chandler asked

Evie a very important question. It was not only important but very unusual for a middle school student to be asked a question like this.

"Evie, would you like to be on a television show for children once a week to help them learn about the sky?" Dr. Chandler was one of the advisers to the television station run by the university. It was part of the nationwide Public Broadcasting System (PBS). At one of the workshops about programs for the future, Dr. Chandler spoke about the importance of science learning for children in elementary school through high school. The board of directors of the television station loved the idea and voted to prepare a proposal for a new television science program.

Dr. Chandler then told the group about Evie's history and involvement with the observatory. He also mentioned how smart and articulate she was when explaining the night sky to other people, especially children. He had even asked her to be part of planetarium programs. Many of the people who came to the planetarium were children and their parents or teachers. It was always a big hit for a child to lead a show so well. Visitors especially enjoyed how Evie was able to inspire them by showing the wonders of the sky and explaining stories about how the constellations were named.

Evie was not at this meeting, but had she been, she would have been blushing and a bit embarrassed by all of Dr. Chandler's nice words about her.

Dr. Chandler had invited some of his fellow board members to one of those programs. After hearing Evie, they agreed that she would be a great choice to be the hostess of the program.

Mom and the next-door neighbors saw Evie smiling broadly. Dr. Chandler's invitation was not a surprise to Evie's mom. She'd told Evie that he had spoken with her about it. He had called earlier to see if it would be all right to bring up the subject with Evie, saying, "Evie would be the perfect choice, but it would ultimately be up to her to decide." Evie knew that her mom trusted her judgment, even about very important questions. This one would be very important indeed!

CHAPTER 8

DAD, MOM, AND THE STAR PRINCESS

Before Evie would agree or not agree to the idea of becoming hostess of a television show, she knew she needed to think carefully about taking on this major work. She knew she needed support from both parents, and she wanted their advice. She spoke to both her mom and dad and asked them to meet with her to discuss the idea. They met at Mom's house and had a long, serious discussion. They talked about the wonderful parts of the star princess idea. Then they went over what each of them thought might be problems they would face if Evie accepted the offer.

Evie spoke first. "This could be the way I can help thousands of children learn to love the wonders of the sky! It would help me meet many people and teachers and see many schools. Perhaps I could add to the army I am trying to create. Evie gave a sly grin. "Who knows? Maybe I might become famous and sign autographs in my spare time!"

On the other hand, it was clear to her mom and dad that Evie was worried. "Will the time I would have to commit to the star princess get in the way of school? Will it cause me to travel too much? Will it add many new pressures to my life, such as memorizing scripts and thinking of new ideas for episodes of the television show? Will it cut down on my time for music and friends?"

Mom added that if Evie accepted the offer, she would have to take specific actions to stay healthy. "When your world changes," Mom added, sounding as much like a doctor as a mother, "some of your habits also have to change."

Evie smiled and said, "I know. I've been thinking about how I will have to eat fewer cheeseburgers, get more hours of sleep, and even exercise." Evie added that last point with a smile and a groan. "It's a good thing I don't smoke cigarettes," Evie added. "I would surely have to quit!"

After all that discussion, and after weighing the good and bad points, both parents asked Evie what she really thought about the idea. She told Dad and Mom that she was very excited about the idea. In her heart, she knew she could do it. Evie went on to say that she was very worried about all the problems that could come up in a very different new life, but she also knew that she could handle those problems because she had a powerful army of people who loved her and supported her. The two most important were Mom and Dad!

After that, her parents looked at each other and agreed that even though they were not married anymore, they would always be united in a strong bond: Evie's happiness. They agreed that with their support and Evie's cooperation, becoming the star princess would be an incredible opportunity. Evie hugged Dad, hugged Mom, and headed for her room to call a few of her best friends to tell them what was happening.

CHAPTER 9

EVIE, THE STAR PRINCESS

Evie heard more details the following week when she and Mom went to the public television station to discuss the idea with the TV producers. They had decided that the program would be called *The Adventures of the Star Princess*. It would start with six shows of thirty minutes each. It would be shown in the morning before most children went to school, and again in the afternoon after school was over. The producers even agreed with Evie's suggestion to simply call the program *The Star Princess*.

Something wonderful was about to happen for Evie—and for young people everywhere!

Evie and Mom began meeting after school twice a week, and sometimes more, with the team of producers, artists, computer experts, and astronomy graduate students assigned by Dr. Chandler. The debut of *The Star Princess* was approaching in just a few weeks! Everyone's excitement was clearly visible. Each program would begin with Evie explaining why astronomy was so exciting and how viewers could use their imaginations simply by looking up in the sky on a clear night. Looking up, reading about astronomy at the school library or on the internet, or simply asking parents, teachers, and friends were all things a *Star Princess* viewer could do.

Each program would include a constellation of the week, and Evie would tell its story. She would describe an ancient myth about that constellation, and she'd also show a star chart and talk about some object inside the constellation. Perhaps it would be a nebula, a star cluster, or a double star. There would be some photos and perhaps a drawings done by a viewer. Evie would interview an astronomer and ask some of the kinds of questions that many of the children listening or watching the program would ask. "How do stars form?" "Do they die?" "How could Chinese astronomers over one thousand years ago see small objects like the Crab Nebula without telescopes?" "How many galaxies are there?" There were endless questions Evie could ask. Part of each program would also find Evie answering questions sent in by children. Every program would end with Evie asking everyone to think about ideas she had learned from Grandpa, Grammie, Mom, Dad, Dr. Chandler, and others.

Each of these ideas was designed to help Evie and those watching to live a more successful life as they grew up and learned more every day. For example, the first episode would end with Grandpa's advice about how very important the whole idea of asking questions was. "Without asking questions, we would never learn and grow." In fact, the question was more important than the answer! Over time, asking questions and thinking about answers or imagining what an answer might be created a spiral of knowledge. More and more information and ideas would come to the people who asked questions, looked for the answers, or imagined what the answers could be. Those weekly ideas from her parents, Grammie, Grandpa, and others would not only end each episode of *The Star Princess* but also lead into the program for the following week.

The television station planned a big campaign for hundreds of thousands of people to learn all about the program. It would invite them all to tune in. There were a dozen announcements about the new program during each broadcast day. Teachers throughout the school systems got information about *The Star Princess* and a little biography about the hostess—one of their own, Evie! There were stories in the newspapers and on TV. As part of the publicity campaign, Evie posed for pictures and was a guest on other television programs. She was interviewed about the program and about her love of astronomy.

Evie was excited to speak to Grammie and Grandpa a couple of times a week. They would always ask her about how the TV show preparations were going and the people she was meeting. They would tell her how proud they were of her, and how they had seen her being interviewed on a TV program or had read about her in a newspaper.

They were also very quick to offer her advice about one of the most important things in life. "Evie, please think a great deal about never becoming so proud of yourself that you forget the importance of being humble and caring about others." Evie's name might become known to many people. Maybe there would even be some *Star Princess* fan clubs in the future. People might ask for her autograph or to have a photo taken with her. Evie knew that Grandpa and Grammie were right. She must always remember that she was very much like all of the other children. If she did become famous, she had a duty to use her fame to make life more fun and better for other people. She must always prevent the serious problem that her grandpa called arrogance. Arrogance happened when one thought one was greater or smarter than one really was. People who are arrogant get into trouble in their lives and hurt other people.

Evie listened carefully and told Grandpa that she understood what he meant. She remembered how, in elementary school, an arrogant person who was a bully had bothered many of the children in her class. She didn't want to become a person like that. She wanted to become a kind person.

Those frequent private conversations with Mom, Dad, Grandpa, and Grammie helped keep Evie on the right track. People began to stop her on the street as she walked with Mom or her friends, and they'd ask whether she was the star princess. When she answered, "I am Evie, and I am sometimes called the star princess," they would often ask for her autograph. She would thank them for their kindness in recognizing her. She would ask children who stopped her to promise to explore their own worlds and to use their imaginations.

By the time the first program was broadcast, the TV station had recorded three other episodes of the show. Evie was always well prepared and had rehearsed. She even helped pick out the clothes she would wear. All of the employees of the television station got to see the first few episodes in advance. They got to meet Evie, who thanked them so much for the help and encouragement they had given to her.

The first *Star Princess* program aired on schedule, and over the next couple of days, the calls, letters, emails, and tweets poured in from children and adults everywhere in the community. They wanted more *Star Princess* stories, and they loved the show. Evie especially loved to read the letters children sent to her, which were addressed to "Evie, the Star Princess." She also loved to read the letters teachers sent in about how the show encouraged students to study science and especially astronomy. Some said they were going to raise money for their school to buy a telescope.

Grandpa had talked with her about what could happen when something became very popular. Strangely enough, that popularity could create problems. Evie was so very busy keeping up with her schoolwork and her music lessons, as well as playing her part on *The Star Princess,* that she didn't have as much time as she wanted to play with her friends and explore other things in which she was interested. Sometimes she didn't have time to practice violin very much at all. Sometimes she had to put off going with friends to the movies or to parties. She had to make sure that they understood that she wasn't avoiding them, and she didn't think she was more important than they were. She had to explain that she promised to work hard on the TV program and in school. Sometimes she had to sacrifice time with them to keep her promises to others, she explained. They all told her they understood, and they kept inviting her to their birthday parties and other events even if they knew that she might not be able to come. Talking with Mom every night about these new pressures and how to balance them helped; so did her conversations with Dad, Grandpa, and Grammie. As a physician, Mom knew a lot about how to help people handle pressure and stress at home or at work, and Evie listened carefully to her advice.

Still, Evie was worried about losing her friends. Both Mom and Dad encouraged her to enjoy time with nature, go for long walks with friends, and enjoy time with others. They thought she would very much enjoy inviting some of her friends to come to the television studio and be with her as she performed. The producers of the television program even suggested to Evie that it might be a good idea for children from different schools to come to the station and be an audience for the filming of each episode.

After about half a dozen episodes of *The Star Princess* were broadcast, it became clear that this program was very popular. Evie's humor and sense of wonder at the night sky shone through. Thousands of children were now watching the show every week.

Other television stations asked about broadcasting the program. Something particularly exciting was announced one day. The national PBS organization worked out an arrangement to make *The Star Princess* a national and even international television program. Students in other countries and students all around the United States, as well as many adults, would get the chance to become regular watchers of *The Star Princess* and great fans of young Evie. She had become famous everywhere as a representative of the excitement that children could feel about science and imagination.

By this time, invitations were pouring in for Evie to visit schools, appear as a guest on other television programs, be interviewed by newspapers and magazines, and even visit observatories around the country. Letters from all over the world arrived. Evie and her mom agreed that she needed a helper and a manager to keep all of this straight. The only rules set down by Mom, Dad, and Evie about what a manager did was that Evie's schedule must leave plenty of time open for fun. Her work must not interfere with her schooling. She must also be able to sit quietly in her room or be outside when the sky was clear. Quiet thinking and imagining time remained very important, no matter how busy she became. She even decided that an episode of *The Star Princess* should be about ideas for reducing stress when children are feeling overworked or overburdened. Evie thought that her own experience would help others.

The Star Princess was so popular that Evie was asked to be the hostess for the next five years. Much had changed in Evie's life. Most of the changes were exciting and wonderful. Evie was even being paid a salary for her work. She decided that she would save most of the salary. However, she also decided that she would use a portion of her earnings to help charities improve the lives of others.

People would write letters and emails to her, thanking her for making a positive difference in their lives and for helping them realize the value of using their imaginations and dreaming. She came to realize how much of an impact she was making for children who watched her program every week. She knew that *The Star Princess* was only the beginning of the career she wanted. She wanted a career that helped educate people, especially children, about imagination and science. She wanted to help them see what they themselves could do to make things better and more fun for their families and for their world.

CHAPTER 10

SCHOOL COMES TO EVIE

It wasn't all that long ago, Evie thought, that she and Mom had had the original conversation with Dr. Chandler about *The Star Princess*. That set in motion the television program, broadcast at first locally and then around the country and the world. Evie wanted to have a career where she would help people learn about astronomy and use their imaginations. However, she had discovered that becoming successful as a young middle school student had a cost, and sometimes a heavy one. As the program became more successful, Evie got more requests to speak to students at schools and conferences, as well as being interviewed for television. Life got more complicated. Evie couldn't walk to school like most middle school students could, and she couldn't go out shopping without being recognized. She talked with Mom and Dad, who also recognized that family life with *The Star Princess* would require adjustments and change.

The family discussed their concerns with the leaders of the television network, as well as with Dr. Chandler. It turned out this was not the first time that the television executives had encountered the need to help one of its rising stars make life adjustments. In fact, they suggested an approach to Evie and her parents that turned out to be a very great idea.

They would arrange for one or more teachers, approved by the school board, to meet with Evie every day, and sometimes on weekends and holidays, to be her tutor and teacher. It was as though Evie was going to be schooled at home, except that the schooling would take place during and after rehearsals and filming of *The Star Princess*, as well as at home. The whole idea was very exciting. Evie could work on both the television program and her education in a way that saved a lot of time, but it still made her schooling fine and fast-paced. The one thing that would be missing would be the chance to be with other students every day. On the other hand, Evie got to spend a lot of time with people her age, not only at home with her neighborhood friends but as she traveled to meet students and teachers from schools in many other places. The idea of a personal tutor was worth trying. Evie said a sincere thank-you to the television network executives for the idea and for caring about her education. In turn, they thanked her for being such an important part of their team. Evie had one request, however, and they agreed. With advice from her parents, she wanted to pick the teacher who would work with her.

Over the next few weeks, Evie was introduced to four different teachers approved by the school board and the television network. These were fine teachers with years of experience in private tutoring as well as in working in school systems. Evie and her parents spent over an hour with each one teacher. They asked questions of the teachers, and the teachers asked questions of them.

Evie wanted to know how the teachers could be flexible in their scheduling of school time, because Evie would be traveling and filming the television program. Filming sometimes involved delays that made it hard to have particular starting and stopping times. Her parents asked about the teachers' approach to education and whether they could teach subjects as diverse as science, languages other than English, history, geography, and music.

All four of these teachers were wonderful. Evie thought to herself that she would enjoy spending time with any one of them. She discussed with Mom who the best choice might be. They both agreed on one particular teacher among the four. This teacher was a lady who not only had great experience but also had a very positive outlook on the world, a sense of adventure, and a very strong sense of humor. She was the youngest of the other candidates; the other three were all retired. The lady made Evie laugh. This teacher could also tell when a particular subject was difficult for Evie, and when it was time for a new approach to the subject. In fact, her new teacher, Ms. Michele Uss, was also very willing and excited at the idea of traveling with Evie as her schedule required. Evie was gaining a new friend as well as a new teacher.

Ms. Uss spoke Spanish and French. Her grandparents had come to the United States from Spain many years earlier, and Ms. Uss had grown up in a family that prized education and the ability to communicate with people from other cultures. Evie thought that this was much like her own family experience with exchange students. If that wasn't wonderful enough, Ms. Uss, like Evie's exchange sister Rita, was an extraordinary piano player. The duets with Evie would happen very often!

The arrangements were made. Evie had a new teacher and a very unusual way of going to school. It was even more unusual after Dr. Chandler suggested to the television network that when subjects came up that might be particularly complicated, or that Evie found particularly interesting, the university would agree to have a professor tutor Evie in that particular subject.

Evie was not the only person affected by the success of *The Star Princess*. So were Mom and Dad! They knew that Evie's success meant travel and pressures that most people her age never felt. Fortunately, Mom had the flexibility to balance her medical practice with being the mother of a famous little girl. Mom decided that she would reduce her medical practice schedule to spend more time with Evie. Dad already had a more flexible schedule. They could both continue their jobs while supporting Evie.

This new form of schooling for Evie involved her own individual teacher, technology like the internet, and her notebook computer. The flexible schedule gave Evie one other great advantage over how her education would have been had she remained in a traditional school. Evie got to move forward in her school work at a pace set by Evie, her teacher, and her mom and dad. For a very bright girl like Evie, who already knew a lot about different subjects, especially science, this flexibility allowed her to excel. She and Ms. Uss spoke Spanish to each other every day, and Evie began studying French as well.

When her schedule allowed it, Dr. Chandler's suggestion made it possible for Evie to attend college lectures in subjects she really enjoyed, like history and archaeology. She met an archaeology professor at the university who had studied ancient astronomy at places like Stonehenge in England. Evie enjoyed learning and thinking about how people thousands of years ago looked at the wonders in the sky. She was able to contrast that with what was happening in astronomy today and what was probably going to happen in coming years. Evie invited her new archaeology friend to appear on *The Star Princess* several times to talk about what it must have been like to look at the sky from around a campfire thousands of years earlier.

Evie officially completed all of the school board requirements for middle school and was more than halfway finished with her high school studies by the time she would have graduated from a regular middle school. With Ms. Uss's continued challenges and encouragement, it became possible for Evie to balance her work as the star princess with a strong and positive educational experience.

CHAPTER 11

MUSIC AND SCIENCE

Working at the Public Broadcasting System opened another wonderful educational doorway for Evie. For years, she had studied the violin even though she had less time than ever before to practice. Still, she would keep up her playing as much as she could. When she traveled, she always carried her violin with her.

She was about to receive a surprise visitor, thanks to her friends at the television network. PBS was very famous for its support of classical music. It broadcast many concerts and performances by world-famous orchestras and performers. Of course, Evie and mom had made it known to network executives how much Evie enjoyed the violin, and how difficult it was to have regular music lessons and practice time.

One day, Evie had a special visitor to the studio where *The Star Princess* was being filmed. The network had arranged for one of the world's greatest violinists and orchestra conductors to come by to meet Evie and talk with her about music. This great violinist was Maestro Hyman Rosenberg. Like Evie, he'd gown up in a family that valued education and music. It was clear to his parents from an early age that their son had a special gift for music and the violin in particular. They went out of their way to create opportunities for him and challenge him to share his talents with others. He was not only a violin virtuoso and orchestra conductor, but he was also an inspiration to millions of people. Evie hoped that in her life, she too would be an inspiration. Like Evie, Maestro Rosenberg had also discovered his lifelong passion as a child, and he'd followed through with developing it.

When he learned of the chance to visit the studio and meet Evie, he was very excited. It turned out that his two young children were avid fans of the television program and watched it every week, often with their dad! The idea that he might meet the star princess herself and perhaps bring home autographed photos for his children was very wonderful indeed.

At the same time, Evie knew about Maestro Rosenberg and had heard him play on recordings and even at a concert a year earlier. She would love the chance to meet him in person and perhaps get an autographed photo of him. Not only did they meet, but they spent a long time together talking about music and astronomy. "Thank you, Evie, for how much you have inspired my children," he told her. "Would you do me a special favor and play a song for me on the violin?" Evie was very nervous at that idea, but after a while, not only did she agree to play a song for him, but they played several songs together. They ended their time together with two invitations they made to each other. Evie invited the maestro's two children to come to the studio with their father and mother and spend some time with her. They could be in the audience for the filming of an episode of *The Star Princess*.

Evie also received a special invitation. Maestro Rosenberg would be leading a concert along with a world-famous orchestra coming to the area in a few months. One of the pieces to be played was a special symphony based on astronomy. It was called *The Planets* by the composer Gustav Holtz. Evie was invited to attend that concert as the maestro's special guest, and she was invited to come up on stage to introduce the symphony to the audience. She was asked to spend a few minutes speaking about the planets so that the audience might have a better sense of what was going on when the stream of the music changed from giant Jupiter to beautiful Venus. Evie jumped at the chance to do this.

She spent weeks listening to *The Planets* and practicing some of the music from that symphony. She also kept in touch with Maestro Rosenberg and visited with him a couple of more times when he was in the area to rehearse for the concert. She did meet his two children, and they came to watch *The Star Princess* being filmed. She had lunch with the kids and even showed them a couple of telescopes that were kept in the studio. They posed for photos together, and Evie happily autographed a photo with each child.

Just as she had hoped, she also got to pose with the Maestro, and she got her own autographed photo of him.

Evie was able to share with the maestro how much she enjoyed listening to *The Planets*, adding that she had been practicing some of the parts. He asked her to play some of the music with him and then helped her improve her playing.

He later called her back with another and very special request. The concert featuring *The Planets* was now only a month away. He asked if she would be willing to sit in with the violin section of the orchestra and join the other musicians in performing part of the work. She was ecstatic and a bit nervous, but she agreed to do it. After all, wasn't that what a brave explorer would have agreed to do when given the chance to discover something new?

It was hard to know who was more excited: Evie, her mother, her teacher, or Maestro Rosenberg. The sold-out concert was brilliantly successful. Evie's fifteen-minute talk to the audience was spellbinding. She combined science with music to explain and describe the planets. She ended her talk by asking that every member of the audience find a child or some person whom they loved, and go out into their backyards in the morning and the evening to find Jupiter, Saturn, Mars, and Venus, which could be seen with the naked eye. When they spotted one of the planets, she asked them to think back to this wonderful night at the symphony. She enthusiastically asked for everyone in the audience who was willing to do this to say, "Yes, I will!"

With that, four thousand people spoke out with a thundering, "Yes, I will!" What followed was loud and long applause not only for how great Evie's little talk was but also because she would be performing with the orchestra. They learned this when she was handed a violin by the maestro and then took her seat with the orchestra.

That night was magical, the music was wonderful, and it became a night that Evie would always remember. She kept thinking that it was possible to tie together music, art, and science. Showing the common ties between science and art would make both of them shine even brighter than they did separately. It gave her a lot to think about, just as she gave the audience a lot to think about.

The concert was broadcast live around the country by PBS. Evie's talk inspired thousands of people to go out and look up at the night sky. Evie went on to invite Maestro Rosenberg to be a guest on *The Star Princess* to help her explain how music and science were connected. He spoke about *The Planets*, and Evie got to speak about what radio telescopes were and how they could actually hear the sounds in the sky.

The excitement of her music adventure encouraged Evie to be even more enthusiastic about learning and pursuing her studies. She also thought about how only a few months earlier, she'd felt nervous and afraid to say yes to the maestro's challenging offer to her. Now, she could look forward to more new adventures and say to herself, "Being brave about challenges, and even looking for them, helps make life exciting and fun!"

CHAPTER 12

PERMISSION TO IMAGINE

Although the violin was Evie's favorite musical instrument, it certainly was not the only one that made her smile. She loved classical music, but she also enjoyed many other types of music, including rock and roll, folk music, and music from other places in the world.

Soon after the wonderful concert of *The Planets* was broadcast on PBS, Evie got a call from two of her very favorite cousins in Los Angeles. Ira Ingber and Camille Ameen were first-class artists.

Camille is an actress who created and cofounded a charity called Inside Out Community Arts. The idea is to use the arts, including writing, music, acting, and graphic arts, to help kids express their feelings. This could be especially important if the children had serious family problems, lived in poverty, or perhaps were the victims of crime. It could also help adults better understand what these kids went through and how best to help them. Camille was very enthusiastic about her work with children and was an inspiration to them. Evie told her several times, "Camille, I am very lucky to have a beautiful and caring cousin." If it was possible to see a person blush on the other end of a telephone call, Evie would see her cousin turning bright red! They would visit whenever Evie was in Southern California!

Ira is a very well-known guitarist and rock musician. He also produced music from his studio and wrote and performed music for TV shows and movies. After recalling how much Evie was inspired by the planet Saturn, he wrote a song that made its way on to one of his recordings. It was called "Enceladus." That is the name of a strange moon of

Saturn, photographed in great detail by a famous robotic spacecraft called Cassini. Evie's love for Saturn, and Ira's own interest in science, made the song come to life.

Ira and Camille spoke with Evie about how music and science, especially as presented by *The Star Princess*, had a common purpose. They gave permission to children, and adults for that matter, all around the world to imagine. By imagining or dreaming, we begin to explore ideas and bring some of them to life. In other words, just as Camille and Ira were close cousins of Evie's, music and science were also close relatives of each other.

Evie thanked Ira for sending her a signed copy of his recording. She thanked Camille for letting her know about Inside Out Community Arts. Evie was already thinking about how that wonderful charity could be featured on a *Star Princess* show! She also started thinking about how she might invite Ira and several of his rock musician friends to appear on the show. Most important of all, she thanked both of her dear cousins for reminding her, just as Maestro Rosenberg had done, that science and the arts are both important tools to make a better world.

CHAPTER 13

EVIE ON SAFARI

By now, Evie was nearly finished with the requirements of the school board to graduate from high school. Her teacher and mentors like Dr. Chandler, and of course her mom, dad, and grandparents, saw to it that she had opportunities to learn and grow as a person.

Even though she was very busy with her television show and the chance to travel and meet children and adults across the country, Evie took special joy in the chance to spend part of each summer with Grandpa and Grammie at their farm. Life seemed to slow down there for Evie. Her visits at the farm gave her more time to dream.

She also learned new hobbies and kept up with her music. Grammie taught her how to knit. Evie proudly showed off the scarf she was finishing as a gift to Grandpa. She was also planning another scarf to go to Dr. Chandler and two more as special birthday gifts for Mom and Dad. She found that knitting gave her quiet time to think and watch as her hands created something warm, soft, and beautiful. She could knit while waiting for the crew of the television show to set up the next scenes in a program. She could knit while riding in a car or on an airplane, or when she wanted some quiet time to think.

The visits each summer to her grandparents' farm was also a time when she could relax and enjoy nature without people crowding around her. She could walk in the pastures with her grandparents' dog, enjoy the beauty of the wildflowers, and visit with friends and neighbors Mike and Margie Conlan's grandchildren, Joshua, Catherine, and Harper.

During her visits with Grandpa, she would still spend clear, bright evenings in his observatory. This time, after years of studying her astronomy books and using several different telescopes, she could point out many more objects in the sky than even Grandpa could. He smiled when he thought back to Evie's first encounters with Angelina, the magic telescope. With his help and Angelina's technology, Evie got to see stars, planets, and objects in deep space like galaxies and nebula for the first time. Their time together sparked the passion in Evie that continued to grow.

Now, years later, here was Evie, the star princess, pointing out new objects Grandpa had not seen before. "How wonderful!" Grandpa told Evie that things had come full circle. Grandpa the teacher had now become Grandpa the student. He couldn't help but enjoy Evie's explanations about astronomy and how confident she had become.

When Evie got back to her studies and life at home, her mom said to her one day, "Your father and I have a special gift for you in honor of finishing high school and your many astronomy accomplishments!"

Evie was curious and excited by this news, however she was also aware that it was really her parents' love and attention that helped her achieve all that she had done so far. She said, "Mom, if anyone deserves a big present for helping me graduate from high school, it is you and Dad!" That wonderful comment resulted in a giant hug and a few tears of love shared between mother and daughter. "So, what's this about a gift?" Evie asked with a smile.

"We have been talking a lot about how hard you have been working, and how wonderful you have become as you have been growing up," said Mom. "We think it is time for you to go on a safari! Your dad will make all the arrangements, and I will be along not only as your mom but also as your roommate and fellow safari guest."

Dad had been telling Evie about the amazing times spent with his special safari guide friend. Grammie and Grandpa were longtime friends of the famous guide, Hayden Elliott. They had met him years earlier when they'd gone on safari in South Africa for the first time. On three more occasions, they had gone on safari with him. Evie nodded, remembering clearly how Grammie had been excited and happy while telling her about the many animals they had seen and the wonderful people they had met. She also showed Evie many photos from their trips. Hayden loved birds and animals, and he knew a great deal about the cultures and the people in South Africa. Dad and Hayden were now working together on their safari business, but Evie had not yet met Hayden.

Mom said, "Evie, we are going on a safari with Hayden! We will see hundreds of animals and birds and take thousands of photos. We will meet people from tribes like the Zulu and the Tembe, as well as people whose ancestors came from England and Holland. Perhaps we will even visit an observatory in South Africa and see some of the deep-sky objects and constellations in the southern hemisphere."

To say that Evie was excited was an understatement. She was jumping around and began asking question after question. Mom often had to say, "I don't know the answer. Why don't you and I get some books on South Africa and start doing some research?"

About two months away from their trip, Evie made a special request to her parents. She asked for one more graduation gift. She thought it would be a wonderful way to say thanks to Ms. Uss if she could come along with them to Africa. Evie's request for a second gift was actually a request for a gift that would be a gift for someone else. "What a wonderful thought, Evie," her mom said. After getting the okay from both parents, Evie told Ms. Uss herself. It made her teacher's day a special day indeed.

Evie told her friends and those she worked with about her special graduation gift. When she told her producers at the PBS station, they all smiled and shared her joy. They were very happy for her because they knew that the two-week safari would be full of educational and fun times for her.

The PBS producers also began to think about some *Star Princess* programs that could be filmed in South Africa. They could teach children about the night sky in the southern hemisphere. They could also mix in stories about constellations involving animals like a lion, an eagle, and a bear. With Evie and mom's permission, they contacted broadcasters in South Africa to begin work on two new *Star Princess* episodes.

Some of the African television stations already showed *Star Princess* programs, especially in schools that used them for science education. Evie looked forward to visiting some of those schools.

Evie wondered if perhaps she could bring some telescopes with her so that the children could see things in the night sky through a telescope they might never have seen before. With Dr. Chandler's help, she contacted several companies that made telescopes. One of the largest companies soon called back to say that they would be very happy to donate ten portable telescopes to *The Star Princess* for her African educational adventure. Evie called the President of the company to thank him for his generosity and to tell him that she would be sure to tell the children and their parents about the company. She would also use one of the telescopes on a *Star Princess* program. That meant that hundreds of thousands of people would see the company's telescope at work.

It was only a couple of weeks after Evie's official high school graduation that Evie, Mom and Dad, Ms. Uss, a television producer, and a camera crew left on the long twenty-hour flight from the United States to the biggest city in South Africa, Johannesburg. Evie had time on the airplane to start work on another knitted scarf. She also read about the animals in South Africa and the southern sky objects. She was looking forward to meeting their guide, Hayden, as soon as they landed.

Mom and the TV producers told Evie that they would be met at the airport by Hayden and some people from the South African Broadcasting System. After their safari, some school visits had been arranged, along with a visit to South Africa's largest observatory.

A long flight covering thousands of miles is something that can make travelers tired and cranky. Not only that, but once they got off an airplane in another country, there were long lines to go through to show their passports to representatives of the government to get permission to enter the country. They also had to find their luggage as hundreds of suitcases were unloaded from the airplane.

When Evie and her friends landed at the airport, however, something unusual happened. The couple hundred people on the airplane all moved in the direction of the customs officers to show their passports after standing in a long line. However, Evie was met by representatives of the South African government and a television crew from the South African Public Broadcasting System. They were there to welcome her and help her move quickly through the government process. Instead of a process lasting more than an hour, Evie went through in less than half that time, and her luggage had already been located for her. She came out into the lobby of the huge airport in Johannesburg with thousands of people moving around and getting ready to travel and arrive in the country. It was quite chaotic.

Evie soon realized that something else very special was going on. Hayden was one of the first people to greet Evie, and he did so with a smile and a big hug. As soon as she came out of the gate, he gave her a safari hat of her very own that had a wide brim to protect her from the sun. He told her how happy he was that they would get to spend some time together, and he promised her many amazing animal encounters. He was ready to explore the wild bushlands with her to find lions, elephants, leopards, giraffes, hippopotami, crocodiles, and still more unusual and rare animals. In typical Evie fashion, she had made a list of the animals and birds she hoped to see. She had already shared her list with Hayden by email. He told Evie he would do his best to work through her list when they were on safari, and he even added some animals such as cheetah and cape buffalo.

The sounds in the airport terminal were louder than usual, and Evie soon found out why. As they moved through the airport terminal, more than one hundred children and adults began dancing and singing. Many children were waving signs that read, "Welcome, Star Princess, to South Africa!" They wanted nothing more than to exchange smiles and waves with Evie as she walked near them.

They were children from nearby schools who had heard that Evie would be coming. They knew that she had been invited to visit their schools and were big fans of *The Star Princess*. The chance to see Evie in person and maybe shake hands with her was exciting and wonderful for them.

Finally, Evie made her way forward, following Hayden's lead to the outside of the terminal and into a large van parked outside. Hayden carefully drove the van out of the city and headed into the bush lands of the game parks for their safari. Evie's African adventure had begun!

Evie's time on safari was amazing. Hayden and her dad delivered on all of the animal sightings on her list, plus a lot more. They visited several famous game parks, including Kruger National Park and the Royal Tembe Elephant Park. Each place they stayed had a main lodge building where meals were served. Every day began with a morning game drive that began before dawn. Evie and Hayden, along with her parents and Ms. Uss, rode in their own safari vehicle driven by a ranger. There was also a small folding seat mounted on one of the front fenders. This was where an expert tracker sat, keeping his eyes wide open for animal tracks and other clues on the road ahead.

There were several vehicles driving around in the game parks at the same time. When one group spotted something wonderful, like a pride of lions, the ranger would contact the other groups via radio so they could come over and enjoy the spectacle. Before the morning game drive began, there were hot drinks for everyone. Evie came to love hot chocolate, especially in the chilly temperatures of the predawn bush. After four hours, everyone came back to the lodge to enjoy a hot meal. They would talk about their adventures that morning, share photos, and enjoy some quiet time or take a nap. After a very long flight and a long drive to the game parks, time to relax and think about what they might see next on the afternoon game drive was very welcome.

In the middle of the afternoon, it was time for another game drive. This one lasted until after dark. The rangers and trackers knew every watering hole and every favorite animal hiding place in the parks. They were also fun for safari guests to get to know. Most had heard of *The Star Princess*, and so Evie often got to ride in the front seat with the ranger. She became very good at spotting game, occasionally seeing something before the tracker could see the animals.

She was the first one to spot a large leopard with an absolutely beautiful spotted coat. Leopards were shy creatures even though they were fierce and strong carnivores. They hid when they heard the sound of the diesel engines of the safari vehicles or smelled the exhaust. They were often the last animals guests spotted on the safaris, and some groups missed seeing them altogether. But not this time, thanks to sharp-eyed Junior Ranger Evie!

Most of the animals ignored the safari vehicles, and they rarely attacked them. Evie asked a ranger why this was so. The ranger said, "Evie, great question! We know that these vehicles are open to the air, like the convertibles you see on the road. They have perhaps six people in them, and we drive right up close to even huge animals like elephants, rhinos, and cape buffalo. You have seen how close we get to lions! But, the animals see one unit no matter how many people are in it. They don't like the smells and the sounds. However, they have gotten used to our vehicles and tolerate us, because we don't every try to hurt them."

"Doesn't it ever get dangerous?" Evie asked as they approached a group of lions lying on the grass only about thirty feet away.

"It certainly can get very dangerous," said the ranger, "but that usually happens because of human behavior. For example, when a person leaves the vehicle, she is no longer part of the unit. Things can get scary when people get too close to a baby animal, especially the elephants, and the mother thinks we are trying to hurt the little one."

Evie realized that the lessons the ranger was sharing with her were also life lessons. "Respect is very important, whether you are a hyena or a person," she said to the ranger with a smile.

"So is listening to the advice and instructions of people who have much more experience than we do," Hayden added.

The excitement of the safari was increased around almost every turn in the road, when animals appeared unexpectedly. Evie took hundreds of photographs, including photos of herds of cape buffalo, elephant, many types of antelopes, huge and fierce crocodiles, lions, hyenas, and even the rare African wild dogs.

Evie later told her friends that the part of her time in the bush she would remember most was the walking safari. As her group got to an open spot in the Royal Tembe Elephant Park, Hayden, the ranger, and the tracker asked everyone to get out of the vehicle. It was time to go for a walk in the bush! For the next hour, led by the ranger and the tracker, everyone went for a hike. Before they left the vehicle, however, they were told about some very important safety rules, such as what to do if an animal came too near. The ranger would warn them about danger with some finger snapping and hand gestures.

As they walked in the bush, the group would stop frequently when the ranger gave them a signal. Sometimes they stopped because a group of elephants was off in the distance, grazing peacefully, and the sight was incredibly beautiful. Sometimes, the ranger stopped the group to look down at some animal tracks or dung left behind by the animals. The ranger showed his guests how to tell whether the rhino dung they found was from a "browser" or a "grazer." He could tell by the food remnants in the dung. He also showed them some different kinds of bird nests and insects.

Evie couldn't help but notice that the ranger was carrying a very large rifle for the first time on their safari. He'd always kept the weapon in the vehicle until now. "Have you ever used that rifle?" Evie's mom asked the ranger.

He replied, "I've been a ranger for over ten years and have never had to fire a shot at an animal. The rifle is a very last resort to protect me and my guests. Even among the animals, respect is a more powerful weapon than a rifle." Evie would remember that important lesson about the power of respect for the rest of her life. She would think back about that when working with her students and her astronomy colleagues.

Finally, everyone went back to the safari vehicle. It was time for a sundowner. That was a tradition that called for everyone to enjoy a snack and a drink as the sun started to set. They saluted the beauty of nature and gave thanks for the adventures they'd had during the day and the friendships they had made!

That final night in the bush was a time for dancing and singing. Hayden invited members of the Zulu tribe to come to the lodge and perform their favorite songs and dances for his guests. He told them that the star princess would be one of the guests, and so some of them brought their children. They had learned about astronomy at school by watching episodes of the television show.

Finally, after enjoying exciting music of the Zulu, everyone went outside to enjoy the amazing clear and dark sky of the African bush. Our own galaxy, the Milky Way, shone brightly. So did the four very bright stars making up the Southern Cross. Evie had read about them and had studied charts showing the southern sky. Now she got to see them herself! She told Hayden that the sky here was amazing and inspiring, just like it was at Grandpa's observatory back home. How she wished he could have come on this safari with her.

Almost at that very moment, Grandpa was looking up at the sky from the front porch of his home. He wondered how Evie's safari was going, and he thought about how great it would have been to be there with her. They were thinking the same thoughts at the same time, but from thousands of miles apart.

CHAPTER 14

THE CHILDREN GET A VISITOR

All of this occurred in the first week of the two-week trip. After this first week of Evie's trip came to an end, she had seen thousands of animals in the wild. Dad flew back to America to return to work. Over the rest of her Africa trip, Evie kept thinking about all she had learned regarding the history, culture, and music of the Zulu. What a remarkable nation of warriors!

Evie, Mom, and Ms. Uss, along with the film crew and producers, went on to the second part of the trip: visiting schools. Most of the next week was spent visiting several schools selected by the government's minister of education, including a school in the area of the Tembe tribe. Evie saw many children and came to realize that many were poor and were not going to a school that was rich with supplies and shiny, new buildings. Even though they didn't have much money, the children at this Tembe school had bright, wide-open eyes and big smiles as they met Evie. Their teachers had been telling them all about Evie's television program, and they got to see several episodes on a small television that was brought to school. They and their parents were invited to meet Evie one evening at the school. She showed the students parts of the night sky and explained some of the things they could see, even without a telescope.

The school was far away from city lights, and so the sky was magnificent. Thousands of stars could be seen. Everyone, including Evie, was amazed at how incredible the night sky looked from Southern Africa. She told the children and their parents stories about how the constellations got their names, but she also asked the children if they knew any stories about constellation names. Indeed, some of them did, and so did their parents. Around the world, different tribes of people in different areas had made up their own stories about the stars.

She called on one of the students to tell her a sky story. That little girl spoke up bravely and told Evie about how the Milky Way came to be. She told of a little girl who became angry when her mother refused to give her some of the wonderful smelling roots she was roasting. In her anger, the little girl grabbed the roots and threw them and the ashes of the roasting fire up into the air. The glowing embers and roots became the stars of the "stars road," as they called the Milky Way—a path through the darkness created by a little girl in the distant past! The little storyteller was rewarded with cheers from her friends and a hug and a photo of the star princess.

Evie was surprised at how very interested these children were in astronomy even though they had no equipment and didn't travel far away from their homes at night. She was happy that she had brought telescopes to share with them.

Partway through Evie's meeting with these children, she brought out one of the telescopes that had been donated. She showed teachers, parents, and children how to use the telescope. Everyone lined up to see some stars and galaxies that Evie pointed out.

Then Evie said to the group, "I am leaving this telescope as a gift to you. I hope that you will all enjoy it and have many hours of learning and amazement by using it. You have been so kind to me. You have taught me much about your own culture. Because of your kindness I'm going to also leave a second telescope in the hope that one can remain at school and the other can be loaned out for students and parents to take home in order to spend even more time with the sky." The first student to get to borrow the telescope was the girl who'd told Evie a story.

As Evie and the people with her who had been filming her visit to the Tembe school headed back to their car, Evie said to the students, "I look forward to meeting some of you later in our lives, and to hearing about how your astronomy adventures may have changed your life, just like it changed mine." With that, there were cheers, hugs, singing, and dancing as the cars drove away. Evie knew she had made a big difference in the lives of the students, but they'd also had a major effect on her.

Next came visits to several more schools in cities like Cape Town. Just outside of Cape Town was the large South African Astronomical Observatory. Of course, everyone who worked there knew about *The Star Princess,* and they also knew that Evie was coming to visit. She got to spend time with them and look through their very large and old telescope.

At each school, she left one or two telescopes for the students and the teachers to use. She did the same thing even at the big observatory, leaving a telescope to be used outside at night for members of the public. The staff at the observatory already had several other telescopes for public viewing, but none that had come directly from the star princess! The staff invited Evie to a beautiful dinner under the big dome and the giant telescope. She had never had dinner with a telescope before! Staff members could bring their children to meet Evie. It was a wonderful evening for them and for Evie, who told stories to the children about how she first became interested in astronomy.

CHAPTER 15

COMING HOME

As the trip was wrapping up, Hayden brought them back to the Johannesburg airport. Evie had a surprise for him. She had set aside one of the telescopes as a gift for Hayden. She knew that he had two sons and that he took thousands of people a year out into the bush on safari. She told him that she hoped that he might take the portable telescope along with him so that he could show some of the southern sky's wonders to his many guests from around the world. With that, there were many more hugs, and the flight home began.

On the airplane, Evie listened to all of the safety information that crew members and the captain spoke about. Of course, she already knew how to fasten her seat belt. Once again, she got a wonderful surprise. The captain announced to the hundreds of people on the big airplane that they were very pleased to have on board Evie of *The Star Princess*. Many of the passengers and crew members applauded. During the flight, even while Evie was knitting a scarf, people came to her seat and asked for an autograph, or they wanted to shake hands and thank her for helping them learn about the wonders of the sky.

All this attention made Evie think back to the advice she got from Grandpa, Grammie, and Mom. "There is nothing more important to becoming a good person than to be humble and not brag. Never think you are better than another person." That advice was something she thought about a lot when people recognized her on the street and get very excited at the idea that they could speak to her and get an autograph.

After they returned home, Evie spent some time organizing the hundreds of safari photos she'd taken in her African safari journal. As she looked at each one and shared them with her friends, she traveled back to Africa in her mind. She relived the wonderful experience of driving around curves on the rough dirt roads and suddenly finding a large elephant or a family of lions right in front of them. Every day on the safari was full of adventures like that.

Her next couple of weeks were spent with the television producers, who had written three more *Star Princess* episodes based upon the scenery and the people Evie had met in Africa. For example, she would talk about the constellation Leo and talk about her lion encounters on Safari. She would talk about the wild dogs of Africa and Canis Majoris, the great dog constellation in the winter sky. These were very popular episodes.

Hayden later sent her an email about what a pleasure it was to meet her and how her visit had inspired not only him but all the people she met, especially the children in the Tembe school. She'd made a big difference in Africa by her kindness and willingness to share her knowledge with others.

Many people, including government officials, visited the schools Evie had seen in the weeks after she left. They were so impressed with the children's joy about the night sky that they created a project to put a portable telescope in every school in South Africa. Her gifts of a few small telescopes led to many more children in many other places being able to see, dream, and become explorers of the sky!

One of the first things Evie did when she got home was to send thank-you notes to people who had made her African safari so memorable. Besides Hayden and the South African Broadcasting Company producer and crew that followed her on her safari, she thanked the headmasters and teachers at every school she visited. She told them how much she hoped the students kept up their excitement about the sky. She hoped their new telescopes would encourage their curiosity. She also wrote to the director and the staff of the South African Astronomical Observatory to express her gratitude for the kindness they showed during her visit to their wonderful facility. She told them how much she hoped to be able to visit again and learn more about the projects they were doing.

Dear Headmaster,

It was a wonderful experience for me to visit your school recently and to meet the teachers and students, whose futures are bright! Their curiosity about the world around them and the joy and smiles they shared with me were inspiring indeed. Please tell them that I will never forget their kindness—and yours! I hope the telescopes they now have at their schools will be used very frequently and will be a tool to help them dream and grow.

Sincerely,

Evie, the Star Princess

Finally, Evie wrote a letter to the President of the telescope manufacturing company that had so kindly donated telescopes for her to take with her. With help from her television network friends, she was able to include a short thank-you video taken at the Tembe school. It showed the great joy and excitement on the faces of the children as they got to see their new telescope and look through it. She thought that perhaps this company and others would be willing to share more of their products with children in the future.

Grammie always stressed to her the importance of seizing every opportunity to say thanks to people who were kind to her. At the end of every episode of *The Star Princess*, Evie would remind everyone watching the program to look for ways to say thanks to people and be kind to others.

CHAPTER 16

EVIE GOES TO COLLEGE

During all of Evie's hard work in her studies of astronomy and the other subjects required to graduate from high school, she always wondered about the next part of her life: going to college. She already knew how important education was to become a well-rounded person. She would talk to her friends about how there was so much information all over the world coming at them constantly. Sometimes it was very confusing to know what was real and what was false. There were movies, TV shows, the internet, video games, music, and so much more. It was no wonder that at times, she and her friends had trouble sorting all of this out. She would talk to her parents and Grammie and Grandpa about all this. They agreed that never in the past had so much information been available in so many different and often confusing ways.

Grandpa helped her think through this problem. "It isn't the information that is important," he told her. "What really means the most is how that information is used to make important decisions." He helped her understand that sorting out the information and using it to create her own future was most important. That was the meaning of wisdom. "People who are truly happy and successful in life are those who search for wisdom and share it with others through friendships, teaching, and being good neighbors and citizens." It was the search for wisdom that would make Evie happy.

In fact, on one summer evening a long time ago in the observatory, while she and Grandpa took photos of a beautiful star cluster, they had a wonderful, quiet time to talk about life. They spoke about how every person passes away at some point, no matter how big, strong, rich, or poor that person might be. Grandpa told her, "What a person leaves behind is what really matters. That doesn't mean a large bank account or a building named after her. What people leave behind—their legacy—is how they will be remembered. Did they help create a better world? Were they thought of by others as mentors or someone from whom others learned a lot? Were they thought of as kind people who shared valuable knowledge? Were they loving people with many friends? This is what a person's legacy is all about," Grandpa explained.

They ended that discussion by realizing that they had just spent a couple of hours taking one hundred photographs of an object called M56, a bright star cluster in a beautiful constellation called Lyra, the harp. The M stood for the name of the person, Charles Messier, who'd observed and created a catalog or a journal (much like Evie's star journal) of deep-sky objects in the eighteenth century. Even though he didn't have the wonderful modern telescopes and cameras, his careful observing and curiosity, combined with keeping notes and drawings about all that he saw in the sky, led to the Messier Catalog, which people were still using and admiring two hundred years later.

Evie thought a lot about the ideas of legacy and wisdom. She imagined and hoped that her role in the future would be to contribute to a better world by sharing her passion for astronomy and for inspiring children. She realized that a big part of creating that legacy was getting as much education as she possibly could.

She was now a high school graduate at age sixteen, two years before most of her friends would reach that goal. Even before she graduated, Evie thought about the next step in her education: going to college. She talked with friends, Mom and Dad, and Grandpa and Grammie to get their advice. She talked to Dr. Chandler and never failed to ask many adults whom she met along the way about their own college experiences. She learned a great deal from them by listening carefully. All of them were happy to give her their best advice and share important moments in their own lives that made them happy and successful. In fact, all of them offered to help Evie with her own college search.

Years earlier, Grammie and Grandpa had helped Evie understand the importance of what Grandpa called "creating your own army." What he meant was that as you meet people along the way and show them kindness and curiosity, they become your friends and want to see you succeed. Sometimes when you really need help with an important decision or a difficult situation, they will be right there. They will have a strong desire to help, even when you least expect it. Evie remembered the many times when her mom would describe very nice patients who came to see her with very serious illnesses. Mom would call other doctors she knew or people who managed large hospitals. She went out of her way to get these patients the help they needed, regardless of whether they could afford to pay. Evie never forgot that important part of wisdom: treating others with respect and helping them.

After looking at the many options she had about going to college, she found that people like Professor Chandler, people at PBS television, other astronomers she had met, and many others were part of her army. They were thinking about ways to help Evie with college. Evie wrote letters to some of the colleges she was interested in attending, but at other times, with her friends' help, she would receive letters from important people at major universities inviting her to apply for admission. She considered the cost of these different schools, their locations, what offers they would make about the use of their observatories for her studies, and scholarships and internships. It was not too difficult for her to narrow down her choices to four or five top universities. She shared her short list with her mom and dad and with Professor Chandler, her good friend who often seemed like a member of her family.

One college stood out in Evie's thinking. That school offered her a place in a special, accelerated doctoral program. It usually took a great many years to earn a doctorate, including four years to earn a bachelor's degree and a couple of years after that for a master's degree. Then it took three or four more years of further study and work to receive a doctorate.

This particular university had developed a program for a very small number of highly qualified students to combine coursework and research. These students could receive all three degrees after seven years. Evie was offered a full scholarship, including living expenses such as housing and meals. They were so interested in Evie choosing their university that she was offered living arrangements at the home of one of the most distinguished astronomy professors in the country. The professor would serve as Evie's adviser, as well as her host, during her time at the university. Evie could work as a research assistant in the astronomy department and have full access to the university's several modern observatories and equipment.

This university was also not very far from her home. She arranged to visit the campus with Mom and Dad. She asked to be able to meet and spend some time with her prospective adviser, Professor Linda Stock. Evie later learned that her adviser had gone to school with Dr. Chandler and that they were longtime friends. He had spoken to her often about Evie and her passion for learning and passing on her knowledge and enthusiasm to others. Besides, Evie already had fans on the university faculty who enjoyed her television programs, even if they were designed for children. Evie's own hard work over the years made her a highly-sought-after recruit for the university. The friends and contacts she had made in creating her army also helped a great deal.

She found her visit to the campus very enjoyable and was impressed with the program and the facilities. Her adviser was friendly and very obviously concerned that Evie should be happy and successful as a student. Evie got to tour the campus with several of the students and ask the many questions about student life at the university. Her student guides also asked her questions about her hopes for the future and her work on her TV show. To Evie and her parents, this university seemed to be a very good match for Evie's continued education.

Evie was also offered the chance to take some difficult examinations before she started as a student, in order to see whether she could get credit for some basic required courses in music, history, English, another language, and the sciences. She studied hard for the next couple of months with help and support from Ms. Uss, and then she took the tests. She ended up with enough credits to be halfway finished with the first-year requirements. Evie was the youngest student ever admitted to the university!

The university was proud to let other potential students and past graduates know that the star princess had chosen to study at their school. Evie was also proud, and she filmed a couple of *Star Princess* episodes on campus about this part of her new life.

It was a hard decision to leave for school even though it was only a few hours away from home by car. Evie, Dad, and Mom agreed that she would be home frequently for holidays and on weekends. Evie's mom and grandparents would also visit her. She would send emails and have regular video chats to communicate with her friends and family.

And so it happened that Evie, the star princess, was now also Evie, the university student. In a few years, she also hoped to be known as Evie, the doctor of astronomy!

CHAPTER 17

TAKING CARE OF EACH OTHER

Even though Evie lived at the university, she chatted with Mom and Dad several times a week. She knew they were her biggest supporters. On weekends, she would visit, staying with Dad one time and with Mom the next. It became harder and harder for her to visit with Grandpa and Grammie at their farm, but she used video chats and letters to stay in touch. She also sent emails to her friend and exchange sister, Rita.

She remembered that while growing up, there were times when it was very hard and confusing to balance her time spent with each of her parents. She could talk to some of her friends about this problem when she'd attended elementary school because many of them also had parents who had divorced. In Evie's case, her parents talked to each other regularly and lived near each other. Whatever difficulties led to their divorce, those things that had separated them gave way to a common and strong bond when it came to doing the best they could do to enrich Evie's life. Evie knew how strong their bonds of love for her were, and that helped her worries about having divorced parents fade away.

As her television show became a great success, they both shared in her joy. When she completed the different stages in her education, they were there, happy and proud of her accomplishments. She knew it would always be that way, and she loved each of them very deeply. She was convinced that whatever great joys or great troubles might be ahead in her future, they would always be a family when it came to taking care of each other.

Evie did very well at school, although she was a bit of a curiosity to the other students. Most of them had seen her television programs and knew that she was very smart and very young. Fortunately, she didn't have much trouble making friends, including new friends who were years older than she was. They went out of their way to help her feel safe and comfortable at the university. In turn, she was kind to them and made them laugh.

When they needed help, she was always there to encourage them. Many of her new friends were not studying science. Rather, they were studying other important subjects like English, psychology, art, or political science. Still, they had to take and pass several science courses to finish their degrees. Evie was quick to help them and encourage them to consider astronomy as their course to meet the science requirements. She found that her enthusiasm for the stars spread to them as well. She enjoyed conversations with them, whether they happened during lunch or while walking to classes. Her friends would ask for her opinion about new developments, like the next space telescopes and space missions, and what they might lead to. Of course, there were always the unavoidable questions about whether she thought there was life outside of planet Earth.

Evie brought with her two of her telescopes and cameras to continue her own personal exploration of the sky. She would invite fellow students to visit her new home and do some observing with her when the sky was clear. Evie continued to play her violin and enjoyed learning about history and many other subjects to achieve her goal of becoming a well-rounded person.

By the time Evie was halfway through her accelerated degree program, she was a teaching and research assistant. She worked with several professors and played important roles in the research projects they were doing. Many of these projects were funded by government agencies, including the National Aeronautics and Space Agency (NASA), the Department of Defense, and even the United Nations. Evie got to do some teaching at the request of some of her professors. Not only did she give some lectures in undergraduate classes in astronomy, but she also volunteered at the university observatory and planetarium to help run stargazing events and meetings of the community astronomy club. Attendance at these events was never higher than when the guest speaker or program guide was the star princess.

Her studies kept her very busy. Her television program had to take second place in her life. Yet during summer and holiday breaks, she would return home and spend part of her time filming new episodes. She also got permission for the Public Television Network to use university facilities to film many of the *Star Princess* episodes. The network agreed that the *Star Princess* programs were so successful and popular that they wanted to continue creating them and they wanted Evie to be involved. They were willing to change the design of the program so that it didn't have to occur every single week, and they also agreed to use some of the dozens of past episodes as repeat broadcasts. All of this allowed Evie to balance her work as a student with her volunteer work in the community and still appear—though now only about once a month—as the star princess on television.

CHAPTER 18

A MOST UNUSUAL REQUEST

The last two years of Evie's doctoral program focused a lot on science education. Astronomy as a science itself was very important to her, but so was the idea of being able to share her knowledge of the sky to educate children. She wondered whether it might be possible to work even harder than she had been and earn a degree in education as well as in astronomy. She shared that thought with her adviser, Dr. Stock, who went on to arrange a meeting between herself, Evie, and the dean of the education department. The subject was whether Evie could get dual doctorate degrees in her two areas of passionate study.

The request to enroll in two doctoral programs at the same time was very unusual. There were hardly any students in the history of the university who were granted that permission. Then again, there was hardly any precedent for a student like Evie to make such a request.

Universities don't change academic programs very easily. In this case, the dean of the education department was aware of Evie's public television program and her contributions to the education of children. He was very sympathetic and listened carefully as she explained why she thought that the two doctoral programs would allow her to pursue her career hopes of making a huge difference in science education. Her adviser met with the dean after Evie left the room. They both agreed that the request was very unique and that there might well be opposition from faculty members in both departments. The dean told Dr. Stock that he could make her no promises about Evie's request, but he would suggest that a review committee be created to formally hear the request. It would make a written recommendation to the President of the university. The committee would have three faculty members from each of the two departments. The university senior Vice President would be the seventh member and be the chair.

It took a month for committee members to be selected, and they set a meeting date. The senior Vice President explained to the other committee members exactly what the request was. Each committee member received a copy of Evie's college records and copy of her biography. First, the committee would hear from Evie herself. She couldn't help but be a bit nervous as she entered a large room in the university library and stood at one end of a long wooden conference table. She was welcomed by the senior Vice President.

She already knew the faculty representatives from the astronomy department, as well as the dean of the education department. Her adviser was in the room to participate in the discussion, but she was not a voting member of the committee. Evie sat down in a large chair at the end of the table and listened carefully as the committee's rules were described. The first question was to be asked by the chair. After that, each committee member would have ten minutes to ask any questions or make any comments they would like with Evie present in the room. Thereafter, she would be asked to leave the room, and the committee members and her adviser would consider the request and make a decision.

The chair of the committee began by introducing Evie to the committee members and congratulating her on her fine academic work and contributions to the university's public relations programs. She helped the university be recognized around the world, even more than it already was, as a leading place to receive a great education. He then asked Evie to explain why the committee should recommend approval of her unusual request.

Evie began by thanking each member of the committee for being willing to consider her request. She assured them that she had not made the request without giving it a great amount of serious thought. She also told the members that she did not make the request out of a sense of arrogant pride or hubris. Rather, she had come to realize that the best way to reach millions of children in the world from hundreds of different cultures was to inspire them to learn the importance of science as one way to make their own contributions. Doing that meant that she must master two subjects. The first was certainly the principles of the fundamental science of astronomy. Her goal, after all, was to use the excitement of this subject and the joy of discovering the wonders of the night sky as a tool for children's larger quest for exploration and inspiration in the world. Astronomy alone was not enough, however. She hoped very much to gain a strong knowledge of the principles of modern education so that she could better translate her science knowledge in a compelling way to those she taught and hoped to inspire.

She added that only by studying at the doctoral level could she associate with and learn from the finest scholars in both fields. She noted she was on track to complete the work for her astronomy degree within the next year, and she felt ready to also join the education department team.

She ended her brief presentation by telling the committee that her time at the university was a time of hard work but incredible joy. It reinforced her passion for life as an explorer of the sky and a communicator with the next generation of students and scientists. She acknowledged that adding an education degree to her academic goals would be very difficult, however she would take the work very seriously. Her focus would be on learning and contributing to the education department's programs. With that, she told the members that she would be happy to respond to their questions.

Each committee member, in turn, began by recognizing her academic achievements and her very powerful work, which reached a huge audience on *The Star Princess* shows. One member asked if she understood that there might be some overlap between the two doctoral programs in subject matter and requirements. Going on to get a doctoral degree in education would take additional study time, even after completing her astronomy degree. She said she understood that clearly. She was ready for the challenge.

She was asked to give examples of how she would use both degrees for the good of her future students. She told the committee that she believed her coursework would give her a focus on preparing study plans and approaches to education for people, not only at the university level but even at the elementary school level. She was interested in working at the kindergarten through middle school level because she believed that this was the best time to create a foundation and a passion for continued learning. The specific example she gave the committee came from her visit to the Tembe tribal school in South Africa. She explained how the children at that school spoke different languages, had different backgrounds, and probably even had different religions. They shared several things, however. One was great poverty compared to what the university students experienced. Other factors were health and family challenges, such as not getting enough to eat, and seeing family members become ill and needing help when that help was not always available. What they also shared was an incredible spirit to learn and share knowledge with each other, as well as with their parents. She would regularly spend time with students such as these in different parts of the world. She would use the knowledge she gained in the education department to be more innovative and sensitive to the students' needs.

Evie was asked about the fact that she would have to complete a long academic paper, called a dissertation. The education department faculty would have to accept it as original and important in the field of education. Had she thought about what that dissertation subject might be?

Evie told them that she had given that a lot of thought. She would lay out a specific, detailed program in her dissertation, subject to guidance from the faculty, to create a "Ten Thousand Telescopes" project. "My project would begin with measuring student science knowledge and behavior, and then I'd put telescopes in thousands of elementary and middle schools around the world," Evie told them. Perhaps a nonprofit educational charity would be the best way to achieve this goal. Perhaps it could even be created as a charitable part of the university itself, with funding from private donors and perhaps government grants.

She cited her experience with the donation of twelve telescopes for her African visit and what a difference those donations made on the schools and on the children. What if twelve telescopes could turn into twelve hundred, twelve thousand, or more? What if each school that received a telescope, or each village where there might not be schools, could have teachers and residents trained in basic astronomy, the use and care for the telescope, and techniques to inspire students? That combination, she believed, could be an innovation that that would change how both science and education for young children was approached.

It would involve subject matter design, creation of the charity, publicity, fundraising, and choosing how and where to make the telescopes available for students. There would also be a measurement system designed to determine whether an increase in student knowledge and improved behavior had resulted.

This possible dissertation subject would be an academic study of education across nations and have a practical outcome. She had a vision, she told the Committee, that her "education in the education department," she smiled, would fit perfectly with her knowledge as an astronomer, to change millions of lives over the years.

Most of the rest of the time the Committee spent with her focused on comments about her dissertation idea and how she could complete the study programs at the same time, without putting so much pressure on herself that she might harm her health. Evie answered with a smile and with confidence, "Over my years of growing up, I spoke almost daily with my mom, a board-certified family practice physician, about ways to maintain a good balance in life. I believe I have been doing that by studying hard academically, balancing it with hobbies such as music, and spending time with friends." She also valued and practiced her communications skills with adults and children in her work at planetariums and schools over the years. There had also been more than one hundred episodes of *The Star Princess*, with much to study and write before each episode.

The committee thanked Evie for bringing her request to them and spending time with them discussing the possibilities. They told her that they would give her request very serious thought and make a decision that day if possible, or take more time to consider the matter. Evie thanked the committee members and expressed her gratitude to them for considering her request.

With that, she left the room. She was able to keep a lunch date at a nearby restaurant with two of her friends, who helped her relax and laugh after her most unusual and stressful meeting.

CHAPTER 19

A MOST UNUSUAL DECISION

The committee adjourned for lunch and met again that afternoon. The chair asked Dr. Stock for her opinion. After all, more than any other faculty member, she knew Evie and knew how the young woman might handle the pressures of working on both degrees. Dr. Stock reminded the committee members that Evie had lived at her house as part of the overall package of scholarships and accelerated degree details that attracted her to the university in the first place. Even now, as a young person in her early twenties, Evie was known around the world for her work in communicating science education to children. She was used to busy schedules and great responsibility. She was used to speaking in front of large crowds to explain complicated subjects. She was always well prepared and had a strong sense of humor. Dr. Stock urged the committee to consider Evie's request favorably. Approval would be good for Evie, good for the university, and good for an entire generation of future scientists and educators.

Committee members from the astronomy department were next asked for their comments. Each said that they had worked closely with Evie for over six years. They had no doubt that she could handle the academic work and that her sense of humor and ability to make friends would be strong assets in succeeding. They also noted that Evie was less than one year away from finishing the requirements of the astronomy doctorate. She had already begun working on her astronomy dissertation. She would qualify, assuming her dissertation passed her committee review, before she even had to begin work on an education department dissertation. They finally spoke about how they agreed very much with Evie that the marriage of expertise in education and in astronomy would be a very powerful combination indeed.

The education department committee members were also very impressed with Evie, but they were more skeptical. They questioned whether she could meet all of the requirements of their program in one year. If she was expecting to graduate in the next year with two doctoral degrees, they could not support the request. However, they also shared the enthusiasm of their colleagues that the combination of success in these two important areas would be very important.

The committee chair said, "Please comment on how much additional study time would be needed for Evie to be able to qualify." They responded that they were well aware of Evie's work in children's education on television; she could receive course credit for that experience. They also knew of her excellent academic record and her status in the astronomy doctoral program. They agreed that considering all that she had already done, an education degree could be achieved in the next two years of work. In other words, she could qualify as early as a year and a half following completion of the astronomy degree.

The committee chair asked if anyone had anything else to add before they voted on the request. There were two other members who had something to add. The first one spoke about how, over the past month, he had gone to three planetarium programs and public programs that Evie had led for the university. He wanted his colleagues on the committee, especially those who were not already familiar with Evie's astronomy studies, to know that both he and his family members who'd accompanied him came away excited and challenged by what Evie had said and how she'd said it. His children proceeded to ask him for astronomy books to study and a telescope as a holiday gift. If Evie could make that impact without formal training in education, certainly her passion to change for the better the future of many children around the world was realistic. He urged his colleagues to think hard about the comments of Dr. Stock earlier that day: recommending approval of her request would be good for her work, good for the university, and good for millions of children.

The final committee comment came from the senior Vice President himself. He said that he thought the idea of a ten thousand telescope project was something that the university President would be excited to support. It could turn into something far broader in scope than ten thousand telescopes—perhaps a hundred thousand telescopes were not out of the question.

With all those comments having been made, everyone took some time out for refreshments and to think about all that they had heard. When they returned, the chair asked if any members of the committee would propose a motion to recommend approval, denial, or modification of the Evie's request.

Several hands were raised by committee members. The most senior member of the education department was called upon first. He reminded the others that he was the one who expressed concern about the request. He said that it was hard to support a significant change in a long-established course of study. It was no different than trying to make changes in the habits of an elderly college professor like himself, who had been used to things being done in a certain way for decades. He had a twinkle in his eye as he made that comment. However, he added that he had come to agree that this case was unique, and so was Evie.

He made a motion that with two conditions, the committee should recommend approval by the President. The first was that Evie would have a two-year time period to complete all of the coursework and dissertation required by the education department. The second condition was that Evie would have to complete her astronomy doctorate in the coming year so that there would be at least one full year of concentration on her education department requirements, plus her education dissertation. If she succeeded, she would be awarded the doctor of education degree.

The chairman asked if anyone would concur with that motion. If there was concurrence by another person, there would be a discussion on the motion and then a vote. Several hands went up seconding the motion. One committee member said that the education department would have to create a doctoral committee to monitor Evie's progress and review her dissertation. All of the members also agreed that Evie's presence at the

72

university brought with it added support from former students and from donors around the country who knew of her work on *The Star Princess*.

It was interesting, they also noted, that Evie was not asking for any special treatment in the sense of waiving requirements or giving her unfair advantages. Rather, she was asking permission to do very hard and prolonged work. They admired her for that and agreed that watching her progress and helping her where they could was the right step to take.

With that, it was time to vote. All seven members voted to recommend approval of the request with the two conditions established by the group. Dr. Stock was asked to call Evie and tell her that the committee had made a decision and wanted her to come back as soon as she could to hear it from them. That call was placed immediately, and Evie was back in the library conference room within an hour.

This time the meeting was short. The chair told Evie that her request was unique and that it challenged them to not only consider her request but think about how they might respond to other similar requests in the future. "Evie," he said to her, "by unanimous vote, the committee is recommending that the President approve your request with two conditions." He spelled those out for her. "The committee agreed that your hard work and your passion for what you are doing is extraordinary and inspiring."

Evie assured them that the conditions were very appropriate, and she completely understood her responsibilities. She thanked them for opening another door for her to inspire, teach, and make a difference. The recommendation would go to the President the next day. The work of the committee had been completed, and the meeting was adjourned.

Early the next morning, Evie sent each member of the committee a note of thanks and gratitude for their support. She delivered her notes in person to the committee members. Now it was up to the university President!

Less than a week later, Evie received a request to come to a meeting with the President. The next day, she found herself in another beautiful office sitting at the end of another large conference table. The President, the senior Vice President, and the dean of the department of education were in the room. The President greeted Evie warmly and assured her that he had reviewed the work of the committee, as well as her academic and community service history.

He made waiting to hear the outcome very easy. He immediately said to Evie, "It is a great pleasure for me to tell you that I have approved your request, as voted upon by the committee." Evie smiled broadly and told the President that she would not disappoint him or the university. The President asked the dean of the education program to arrange for Evie to meet with a faculty member who would serve as her education degree adviser. This person, Dr. Timothy Harris, would work out the details of her dual enrollment and the coursework she would be required to take. The meeting ended.

The President asked Evie if he might make a personal request. Evie said, "Gladly!" The President told her that his young daughter, Juliana, was an avid fan of *The Star Princess*. She had attended several of Evie's planetarium shows. She wanted very much to have her own telescope and he knew nothing about what kind to buy. "Evie, would you be willing to give me advice on the best telescope to buy for Juliana?"

Evie not only assured him that she would be very happy to do that, but she went on to suggest that it would help make Juliana's experience even better if she could meet with Evie and discuss her interest in astronomy directly.

What followed was a dinner invitation from the President. Immediately Evie's mind raced back to that time years earlier when her own interest in astronomy was excited by not only a visit to Grandpa's observatory and meeting Angelina the magic telescope but the evening at home when Dr. Chandler came to the house for dinner. He then talked to Evie about astronomy. Evie now had the opportunity to give back by helping inspire the President's daughter. Juliana seemed like a younger version of Evie, excited to learn about the sky and very happy indeed to have someone like the star princess as her personal guide to learning.

CHAPTER 20

"DOUBLE DOCTOR" EVIE

As Evie promised she would, she spent the next year working very hard to finish her astronomy dissertation. She chose a topic approved by the faculty about an incredible development in the study of the sky: the discovery of exoplanets.

For thousands of years, people thought that Earth was the only planet in the universe. However, about five hundred years ago, the first telescopes began to appear. This led to the discovery of other planets orbiting the sun. They were part of our own solar system. Discovering and coming to understand planets like Venus, Mars, Jupiter, and Saturn helped expand the way people thought about the universe.

About twenty years ago were the first discoveries of planets orbiting around stars that were not part of our solar system. Those were the exoplanets. Wonderful instruments such as the Kepler Space Telescope helped scientists discover thousands of other planets around other stars. The equipment was getting better and better every year. Evie would participate in a further expansion of our thinking about the universe. She chose to focus on whether exoplanets had atmospheres. If so, what might those atmospheres be like?

She designed studies and got permission to use equipment, including time spent on very large telescopes. She even got permission to use one of the world's largest telescopes, a new one located high in the Atacama Desert in Chile, called the European Very Large Telescope. Getting permission was perhaps helped a bit by her exchange sister Rita recommending it. Rita had by now taken over leadership of the construction company founded by her father. Her company, Evie knew, had built the European Very Large

Telescope in the first place. Evie certainly didn't ask for her help and didn't even know that Rita asked on her behalf. However, Rita was part of Evie's army and knew it would be a great help to her to get some telescope time. Grandpa was right: one might never know when one's army would come to one's aid!

Her research goal was to determine how to detect atmospheres and what chemicals they might contain. After more than a year of hard work and innovative thinking, she reached the conclusion, supported by scientific data, that many, and perhaps most, of the rocky, earthlike exoplanets had atmospheres. She theorized that those atmospheres looked like the ones found in our solar system. The chemicals in those atmospheres were likely to be similar to the ones around our familiar planets. Evie developed research methods to study the small amount of information available about exoplanet atmospheres and how to refine those methods. Evie went on to suggest that several of these planets had atmospheres with large amounts of oxygen and nitrogen gases, just like Earth.

Finally, after all her hard work, her well-written dissertation, and a compelling presentation about the dissertation to the faculty members who had to review and approve her work, a wonderful thing happened.

On the morning of graduation day at the university, Mom, Dad, Grammie, Grandpa, Dr. Chandler, and many of her friends sat in the huge auditorium ready to cheer (and perhaps shed some tears of joy) as the announcer called Evie's name. She slowly walked across the stage to the shouts of the huge audience. The graduates knew her as a fellow student, as a friend, and as the star princess. Though she began her walk across the stage as Evie, the graduate student, she knew that the journey across the stage was only a short one. However, the path to leave the stage as Evie, a doctor of astronomy had been a long and very rewarding one.

The week after graduation, there was a big party in her honor organized by her family and friends. Soon after the party, Evie could be found hard at work in the education department. This time her goal was to become "Dr. Dr. Evie." It would take at least another year for that double dream to be realized.

Evie spoke at several astronomy conferences to present her paper about exoplanetary atmospheric conditions. She also continued to visit schools and do *Star Princess* episodes. Now, however, those episodes were fewer and fewer because she had so many other projects going on. The television network understood that all things change. The weekly episode became monthly and then only as periodic special presentations.

CHAPTER 21

PROFESSOR EVIE

Much of the new doctor's time at the university was spent in the education department taking doctoral classes and beginning work on her next dissertation. One day, however, she got a message asking if she would kindly attend a meeting with the dean of the astronomy department.

The subject of the meeting turned out to be a surprise to Evie. The dean told her that in the next school year, the department would be adding a faculty position. The dean asked Evie to accept an offer to join the faculty as an assistant professor of astronomy! She would focus primarily on teaching undergraduate students.

She could hardly contain herself. It was exactly the kind of work she hoped to do. She could continue her research while teaching and inspiring the next generation of scientists. She would also be able to expose students who were not studying science to all that was going on in the world of astronomy. Every student at the university had to take several science courses as part of their studies. She hoped that many would choose astronomy for that requirement. She would be able to continue helping younger students develop their own individual passions just as she was able to do.

Her response to the dean was enthusiastic but also realistic. She told the dean that she would love to join the great faculty and would work with her education department colleagues to try to determine how that might be possible in the coming year. She would still be working on her education dissertation, and she could not yet commit to full time faculty work until that was completed. The dean assured her that her teaching work would be reduced while she finished her education program. He also confided in her that he had already talked to the dean of education privately to tell him what he wanted to say. The dean of education felt confident that Dr. Evie could be the new assistant professor of astronomy while also moving toward becoming a double doctor. Under those circumstances, Evie said she felt honored, humbled, and thrilled to become a faculty member!

Life was more complicated for Evie over the next year. She had already scaled back on her commitments to *The Star Princess*. The program had become a periodic television special and would appear three or four times a year. She no longer had classes to take. Now she had classes to teach! Her dissertation for the department of education was finally completed, presented to the faculty, and approved. She could now complete formal work on the Ten Thousand Telescopes project she had begun as part of her dissertation. She would also teach several classes in the astronomy department and do occasional television program specials. She hoped she could continue the joy of playing her music and spending time with her many friends.

CHAPTER 22

EVIE OF THE TEN THOUSAND TELESCOPES

While working on her dissertation idea about ten thousand telescopes, Evie knew that she needed sponsors and supporters to reach the goal. She planned a campaign carefully: people to contact, creation of a nonprofit foundation, proper accounting for donations, completing required government paperwork, publicity, and more. Of course, she had to select the best, most affordable telescopes for the project, as well as the best places to make the donations. She also needed to design a training program for the teachers at each school. All of this was a huge task that required much help. It was time to reach out to Evie's army!

She gathered a group of friends and colleagues she felt would share her passion for the idea and commit to help. The university President would be part of the effort, as would the attorneys and accountants for the university. It took about three months to make the foundation idea a reality because she found a way to simplify the process. She got the existing university foundation to create a separate educational fund called the University Star Princess Ten Thousand Telescope Charitable Fund. The university foundation already had all of the legal and fundraising concepts in place. The Public Television System helped with publicity, including asking its wealthy donors for help to start off the project. In turn, PBS would be allowed to film some of the presentations of new telescopes to the schools and document what happened afterward as students and teachers got to use the new equipment.

Evie contacted telescope makers and got recommendations about the most likely kinds of telescopes: small enough to be portable, very high quality, very affordable, and easy to use and maintain. She hoped to also get cameras donated along with solar filters for looking at the sun, as well as computerized mounts to make the telescopes easier to use. Several companies responded excitedly. Finally, she selected two companies to supply the telescopes, and with help from other astronomers, she negotiated very low prices.

The companies asked permission to include their support for the Star Princess Fund in their advertising, along with pictures of the telescopes being used. They weren't being completely charitable in offering to supply telescopes. They knew that the publicity and putting thousands of their telescopes in schools would encourage many more to be purchased by parents for their kids. They even offered to name the telescope models the Star Princess Telescope Series. Each telescope package would cost about $800. The companies agreed to help get the project under way by donating one hundred telescopes each.

To Evie's great joy, several very wealthy people who supported the university and PBS quickly called to help. Top executives from the university also joined in. Ten thousand telescopes would cost $8 million. However, with some very large early donations, grants from school districts around the country, gifts from corporations, and even an educational grant from NASA, all the money needed was raised within two years. Hundreds of thousands of children were watching the night sky and marveling at the sun thanks to Evie's idea and the help of many friends.

CHAPTER 23

EVIE THE POPULAR

There were many professors at the university to help the thousands of students working on their degrees. In any major university, there are hundreds of subjects available for students to explore as they think about their futures.

Dr. Evie realized how fortunate she was to have found a passion for a subject like astronomy at such an early age. Over the years of teaching that followed, Evie still saw many students getting close to graduation but not yet knowing what they really wanted to do for their careers and for their lives.

That made it all the more rewarding for her to teach "Introduction to Astronomy" and "Advanced Astronomy" for undergraduate students surveying the field. She hoped that she could help students find their way into an exciting career in science, just as Grandpa had helped her twenty years earlier.

Evie was a great lecturer who could explain complicated ideas clearly. She could explain them in a way that made them come to life for her students. She could also explain them with a sense of humor and a sense of how one part of astronomy could relate to another part. She emphasized that studying the universe related to other subjects like mathematics, philosophy, and history.

It was no wonder that her Astronomy 101 class was extremely popular and always crowded, even for students who didn't think they would do well in a science course. Although her classes were full, Evie enjoyed the chance to work with many of her students individually. She liked the part of her teaching that occurred after class. That was when groups of students would wait for her to leave the classroom to stop her in the halls. They would ask questions about where they could get more information about something they saw in the sky or had read about. Some would ask if she would help them with some project they might be working on. Grandpa had ignited an interest and a passion in his granddaughter. Now it was Dr. Evie's turn to pass on that tradition and excitement to another generation of curious students. She hoped that some of them would continue their astronomy studies and choose to be explorers of the sky just as she had done.

Professor Evie was very popular, teaching undergraduate students as they worked on getting their four-year college degrees. Advanced students of astronomy also sought her out to mentor them as they pursued their own dreams to become a doctor of astronomy and maybe work for a university or a government agency. She was happy to work with the students, and in turn, they were happy to be able to have her as a coach and a research director.

Her fame stretched beyond the university. She was asked repeatedly to be a guest on television programs and radio broadcasts to comment about events in astronomy or science in general. She was a guest speaker at conferences and often went to elementary schools and high schools to speak to young students about the amazing things they might find by looking through a telescope or taking up astronomy as a hobby.

Although Evie was not in charge of the university's planetarium or its observatory, the other faculty members were always happy to welcome her when she came in to use the tools of the university, such as large telescopes, cameras, or powerful computers to do her own research. She also enjoyed being a guide for distinguished visitors and possible future donors who wanted to see some of the wonders of the sky and specifically asked for her.

At one large scientific conference held by the university, Evie gave the keynote lecture about a particular subject she found very exciting. She remembered clearly her first sight of the ringed planet Saturn through Grandpa's telescope. She remembered how stunningly beautiful Saturn was, standing alone in a dark sky with its rings wrapped around it like a shining belt around the waist of a knight in armor. Since that adventure as a child, Evie took every opportunity she could to show students this amazing sight. Saturn was her favorite object in the sky. She spoke that day with passion and excitement about what it might be like to visit Saturn and its moons. She mentioned the latest findings about the atmospheres around some of its moons. She wondered what secrets that huge planet and its moon family might hold.

In fact, Dr. Evie always talked about the importance of asking questions in science. It was the questions and the wondering that directly led to proposing theories and conducting experiments and research. That scientific research could very well lead to new discoveries which could help every human being on Earth. She often said it was ironic that by studying things not of Earth, the greatest contributions to the betterment of Earth might result.

CHAPTER 24

THE SON GETS BRIGHTER

Evie could not have known about two particular people in the audience that evening. They would play a very important role in shaping the rest of her life. These two people took many notes during her speech and were particularly fascinated by what she said and how she said it.

One of the people was the deputy director of NASA. Deputy Director Ernie Rossi was to be a presenter on the next day of the conference. He would discuss the many projects and plans for exploration that NASA was developing. He would ask the hundreds of people attending the conference to join with him in helping make those plans come true. He knew that money for any big project was in extremely short supply. There were so many worthy projects, and there was fierce competition about which ones would be funded and which ones would have to wait for years longer. Many would never be funded at all. He knew that one of the best ways to help convince other people, and especially members of Congress and heads of corporations, about the value of research and exploration projects was to have people actively supporting them. He pointed out that scientists in particular needed to be leaders in clearly explaining what could come from the research. After listening to Evie's speech, he kept thinking that she could be one of those people. She could make plans for future space exploration come alive for people once they understood how important the results could be for the betterment of everyone on Earth.

The second person sat in the middle of the crowded auditorium trying to blend in with the crowd. He was a young student in Evie's astronomy class the prior year and was named Shane. This young man was one of those students Evie hoped to inspire. He would later say to Evie, "You touched a nerve in me through your lectures. You opened a doorway in my imagination that led me to consider astronomy as a future career. I will always thank you for that inspiration." Shane began to read as much as he possibly could about the subject and about what kind of telescope to buy. His hard work earned him an A in the class. As was her habit, Professor Evie wrote a short note to him congratulating him on his grade and encouraging him to always keep learning and asking questions.

Dear Shane,

I sometimes write notes like this one to a few students who have done exceptionally well in my classes. You are one of those students. I congratulate you on working hard to appreciate the beauty of the universe and being curious about what makes it tick. I hope you continue to pursue astronomy and science in general. Please know that you have much to contribute to the world if you study hard and imagine great possibilities.

Sincerely,

Professor Evie

There was something else about Shane that Dr. Evie had rarely encountered before, despite the thousands of students who had been in her many classes. Shane was never alone in class. He was always accompanied by several men and women paying great attention not to her lectures, but to Shane and to those around him. In the past, she had had several students whose families were extremely wealthy or were the children of ambassadors or rulers from various other countries. Those students were sometimes accompanied by rather obvious bodyguards. However, those with Shane were very subtle and tried hard to blend in with the students. Faculty members were told that the son of the Vice President of the United States, Mr. Charles Albert Broxton, was enrolled at the university. That was Shane.

With his own record of hard work and good grades, with help from his parents and friends, and with a copy of Dr. Evie's encouraging note, Shane was allowed to volunteer as an unpaid intern at one of the world's most famous observatories, the United States Naval Observatory on Massachusetts Avenue in Washington, DC. It was a short walk from his home. In fact, he actually lived on a street called Observatory Circle.

Every day when he got home, he would chatter excitedly to his parents and friends about the news of the latest developments in astronomy. He told them what he did that day at the observatory and how much he loved the subject.

The US Naval Observatory was founded in 1830. Its major original functions had to do with navigation and time keeping. Ships came to rely on charts of the sky to help them arrive more accurately at their destinations. People all over the country relied on the official time kept by the observatory staff. Now, in addition to these important duties, the observatory was a major research institution, just like Dr. Evie's own university.

Shane invited his father and mother to come to the observatory so that he could show them around and allow them to see what he did every day as an intern. If they would like to do that, he promised to arrange for them to also meet the director of the observatory, Dr. Matthew Kramer, while they were there.

His parents were very pleased about the excitement Shane showed at finally discovering a wonderful interest. They would be very happy to visit him, although it would take several days, perhaps weeks, to arrange the visit. Schedules had to be adjusted, and police officers and secret service agents had to be involved in planning for the safety and security of the Vice President.

Vice President Broxton was a lawyer and had been a corporate executive in a technology company before being elected to office. His former company made the latest, fastest, and most powerful computers and was doing quite well. However, Vice President Broxton could no longer be involved in the business of the company. He had left his position years earlier to run for election as a state representative and then as a member of Congress before being elected Vice President. Although he did not have much direct knowledge of astronomy, he certainly understood the power of technology.

He also understood the great and positive changes in his son Shane as he grew more confident and knowledgeable about his future career. Shane spoke repeatedly about his wonderful professor and his inspiration, Dr. Evie.

Finally, the Vice President and Mrs. Christine Broxton made the trip down the road to the big observatory run by the United States Navy. They had dinner with Director Kramer and several of the astronomers and officers at the facility. They learned of the many research programs under way at the observatory that could lead to breakthroughs in our understanding of the universe. Their nineteen-year-old son was nervous and proud as he acted as tour guide for his father and mother. He showed them where he worked, introducing them to the other observatory interns and their supervisors. He particularly enjoyed showing them what his assignments were all about.

The US Naval Observatory had large, powerful telescopes and the best available scientific instruments to explore the heavens. However, what they really had was the incredible enthusiasm of scientists and interns who couldn't wait to come to the office each day to see what might result from their work. Of course, being in the middle of a large city meant that the seeing was harmed by all of the lights in the area. For that reason, the observatory also operated a dark sky facility in Arizona, where the very large telescopes were located and where ambient light from cities and towns was minimal.

During the tour, the Vice President mentioned how excited his son was to be working in the observatory, even though he was volunteering and received no pay. He also mentioned the impact on his son of this college professor and astronomer at the university very far away. The director of the observatory had never met Evie, but he knew of her work and had read some of her papers. He commented she was such a clear writer that even complicated scientific papers were made more interesting and understandable.

CHAPTER 25

THANK YOU, MR. VICE PRESIDENT

Grandpa had told Evie long ago, "Sometimes our lives are shaped by events or coincidences that we do not plan and that end up surprising us." That's what happened in the weeks, months, and years that followed Evie's astronomy conference speech.

One rainy evening in Washington, DC, months after the university astronomy conference and Evie's keynote speech, the deputy director of NASA called in a small number of his closest advisers, including Director Kramer of the US Naval Observatory, to discuss a new and very important project. There was an unusual nervousness in the deputy director's voice as he described how this project was to be treated with great confidentiality and was not yet ready for discussion with anyone else. He emphasized the word *anyone*. This was a project with the potential to answer the greatest scientific, philosophical, and religious question ever asked by human beings.

The project had not been officially named yet. No one had yet been chosen to be the head of the project. So far, it was simply called Ice-E, referring to ice detected on Saturn's moon Enceladus. It would need just the right person to lead the effort if it was to succeed. It was a project that would cost a huge amount of money and would require cutting-edge technologies, some of which did not even exist yet. It would be competing with many other programs in other government agencies for funding. The project would have to be supported strongly by Congress, by the President, by the scientific community, and ultimately, by the entire country and beyond. The project would involve scientists from around the world. He believed that the approval would come if people could only understand why it was so important.

The person who could lead this kind of huge project successfully had to be a scientist, an administrator, a budget director, and (perhaps the biggest part) an extraordinary campaigner. The very important campaigner part of the job would be the key to getting the project approved in the first place. The public's imagination would have to be fired up to support with enthusiasm a great new exploration. How could this complicated idea be explained in such a clear and compelling way that scientists from all over the world would want to join in? How could the enthusiasm of students and schools throughout the world be ignited so that they would want to follow along and feel that they were a part of something amazing? Even Congress, the President, and other government agencies competing for funds would have to become strong supporters of this new initiative.

Finding a leader of great credibility, of great caring, and of great communication ability would not be easy. However, it was the only way to ensure success for the project.

The purpose of this meeting, presided over by Deputy Director Rossi and Director Kramer, was to create a short list of people who could do such a job. That short list would be narrowed down to one or two people who would be recommended to the director of NASA, the President's science adviser, the national security adviser, and ultimately the President himself, who would make the final selection.

There were several very distinguished scientists whose names were discussed. They were all brilliant and were well known as some of the greatest astronomers in the world. However, would the scientific community rally around any one of those people? There were also grave concerns about whether the public would also trust the project leader and provide excited support.

As they neared the end of the two-hour brainstorming session in NASA's executive office, Deputy Director Rossi said to the group, "I would like your opinions about one additional name to be on the short list." He then mentioned Dr. Evie and how impressed he'd been with her leadership ability and persuasiveness when he'd attended a conference at which she'd delivered the keynote address. Director Kramer said that he had never met

Evie, but he was also well aware of her ability to inspire others. They also mentioned the fact that the Vice President was very much aware of the positive impact she could have.

Finally, by the time the meeting ended, the list of possible directors for this major new project was narrowed down to Dr. Evie and two other distinguished scientists. Evie was the youngest candidate at thirty-nine years of age. She also did not have direct experience managing any endeavor as large as Project Ice-E. Then again, no one did! It was beginning to look like a selection contest between relative youth and persuasiveness versus the greater experience of older scientists.

Over the next few days, important things happened with a strong and growing sense of urgency. First, the details of the project were sketched out in a three-page briefing paper that was reviewed and approved in concept by the director of NASA and the President's science and national security advisers. "Approval in concept" did not at all mean that the project would become real, or that it would receive support or funding. What it *did* mean was that the idea was so important, it was considered worthy of being created. Rossi and Kramer could sense that there was a special importance attached to this project, and they focused great attention on it as a result. Yet even they were not sure why they had that feeling.

The other development was that the three people on the leadership short list for the project became the subject of a great amount of work by several government agencies. These agencies, including the FBI, NASA, and members of the staff of the Vice President, assessed the backgrounds of the three candidates to make sure that whoever the President appointed would serve with honesty, ethics, and commitment, as well as technical knowledge. These background checks were essential for anyone directing so major a task. The background checks would also be necessary to determine whether anyone on the short list should be removed from consideration.

In fact, that was exactly what happened with one of the three candidates. That candidate's past work history, despite his brilliance, was full of conflict and confrontation with others. Whoever directed the new national project would have to build support and agreement, rather than increase tensions. The new leader should not be a person whose attitude or behavior would create a situation in which highly respected people from many countries and with many different backgrounds would be driven from their jobs by feeling disrespected or badly treated by someone acting like a bully.

As staff members considered nominees to important positions like judges or cabinet members, the President had said, "The best people to do important work are not necessarily the smartest people in a particular subject. They are also often not the people who receive the most pay. The most successful people are those who are the happiest about the work they do and feel appreciated and recognized by others. The best leader is the person who can create a work environment in which other people feel valued, full of hope, and have the expectation of success. The best leader needs to be not only very smart and articulate but a great teacher." On all of these counts, Dr. Evie remained one of two very strong candidates. So far, however, neither person had any idea about what was about to be asked of them.

With Project Ice-E being approved in concept and the short list to head the project narrowed to two people, it was time to meet directly with the two candidates to explain the project. It was time to see whether they were available and interested, as well as enthusiastic and ready to make a major career change to full-time leadership of something that could astound the world.

CHAPTER 26

SPECIAL MEETINGS—SPECIAL SECRETS

Later that week, the directors of NASA and the US Naval Observatory sent special representatives to meet privately and separately with the candidates. In Evie's case, these emissaries attended a couple of the lectures in her undergraduate astronomy class, sitting near the back of the auditorium. They came up to her after one of the classes to ask if they could speak with her in private on a matter of very great importance. They showed her their rather impressive credentials, including badges and photo identification cards, and they asked if it would be possible for her to come to Washington, DC, right away to meet with their bosses. They told her that they were not able to explain why they were making the request at this point, because the subject was extremely important and highly confidential. They had made all the arrangements for her travel and assured her that at this meeting, all the details of the reason for their request would be made clear. The same message was also delivered to the other candidate.

This was the most unusual invitation Evie had ever received. It was full of mystery but also made her very curious about why two of the most important and famous professionals in Astronomy would seek her out. She accepted the invitation, arranged for another professor to deliver the next few of her classroom lectures, and was soon on an airplane bound for the airport in downtown Washington, DC. Once there, she was met by an escort officer from NASA who had already arranged for her luggage to be taken to what she thought would be a hotel.

As they left the airport, the escort officer handed her a dinner invitation from the director of NASA, Elyse Porter. Dinner would be with a small group of people, including the director of the US Naval Observatory Kramer, and NASA's Deputy Director Rossi. She went on to read that the dinner was to be at the Blair House.

She knew the Blair House was the nation's official guest residence, and it was near the White House. She was looking forward to visiting that famous residence. What she could hardly believe, however, was that her government car drove right up to the front entrance of Blair House. After a security check, she was shown to her rooms. She would not be staying at a hotel like she'd thought. She was to be a guest at the Blair House itself! She was also invited to a brief tour of the US Naval Observatory before the dinner. She ate a quick bite of her favorite snack, blueberry yogurt, which she'd found waiting for her in her room. Then she finished dressing for dinner just as her NASA escort officer arrived to take her to the observatory.

Evie knew that the US Naval Observatory was one of the greatest astronomy facilities in the world. That was why she'd gratefully accepted the invitation to visit. She was not able to meet Dr. Kramer at the observatory, however. She did meet several of the astronomers as well as the summer interns. To her surprise, young Shane was one of them. She remembered how well he had done in her class and the note she'd written him. Obviously, he had followed through on her advice. She still had no idea that she had so profoundly influenced him.

The two-hour visit seemed to fly by very quickly. It was time to go back to the Blair House. She was again escorted through security. She and her NASA escort officer were now joined by two Secret Service agents as they escorted her into a reception area near the dining room.

Just before dinner, Director Porter and Deputy Director Rossi came into the reception room, shook hands with her enthusiastically, and welcomed her to Washington, DC. They told her that they were so glad she had accepted their invitation, as unusual as it was. They also told her that they knew she must have many questions about the mystery surrounding her visit. They assured her that by the time dinner and dessert had concluded, she would fully understand why she was there.

They were then joined by Director Kramer of the US Naval Observatory, who thanked her for visiting the facility. He went on to say, "I hope you forgive me for not being there in person to greet you for the tour. I had a higher calling as a daddy to be at my nine-year-old daughter's first violin recital!"

Evie understood and agreed that being at his daughter's school late in the afternoon for her first recital was a most important reason to miss a meeting. Everyone smiled as they were asked to come in to dinner.

They were shown into the dining room, where they sipped wine and had some appetizers before dinner. Evie rarely drank wine or any other alcoholic beverage, but she enjoyed sipping a bit of prize-winning white wine from California, the home state of the Vice President—and the location of her university.

As if on cue, the door to the dining room opened, and in walked the Vice President of the United States and his wife, Christine. He walked directly toward Evie, reached out his hand, and warmly greeted her. Mrs. Broxton gave her a hug and welcomed her to Blair House. A slightly nervous Evie said, "It is a pleasure and honor to meet you both, even though I don't really know why I am here." That brought smiles to the faces of the people in the room.

Christine Broxton, who had also been a teacher for many years, proceeded to thank Evie very much for all she had done for their son Shane. Evie replied, "My hope as a teacher was that I might also influence young people to find a path in life which would make them happy." The Vice President smiled and nodded.

They mentioned that their son had so thoroughly enjoyed her undergraduate class and was so taken by what he'd learned that he had turned his bedroom into an astronomy laboratory. His parents told her that she had been the catalyst in helping him make a career choice. She was his inspiration and his role model, perhaps without her even knowing it.

She blushed at the compliments and the sincere gratitude expressed to her. Evie had always been a humble person. She appreciated compliments, but she tried to focus attention on other people's contributions. "As you already know, your son is a fine young man and could become a great astronomer. He has already shown that he is a superior student, and perhaps most important, he is great at asking questions during and after class." She went on to mention with a smile that they didn't have to invite her all the way to Washington, DC, to thank her! Again, everyone laughed and smiled. The Vice President told her that she had been invited for another reason, which she would soon discover.

The Vice President told her just before dinner, "It is sometimes hard to understand that in life, it is often much more important to ask questions than to give answers. This is especially true in science. It is questions and wondering about why things are, or appear to be, that leads to experiments, ideas, or theories—and discoveries. These, in turn, lead to new questions. The power of the question is immense."

Wow, Evie thought. *He must have been talking to Grandpa!*

They sat down to dinner at a beautiful table with china dinnerware emblazoned with the seal of the Vice President of the United States. Evie was amazed at how wonderful the food tasted. From the salad to the dessert, the dinner was a gourmet delight. Every course was superb. She loved every one of them. In fact, she smiled as she pointed out that the Blair House chef must be a mind reader, because the chef seemed to have only served foods that were her favorites. She made it a point to ask if the chef could come out of the kitchen so that she could thank him in person. That act of humility and thanks impressed everyone at the table, including the chef.

Evie would later learn that her favorite foods, including blueberry yogurt in her room as well as the dinner menu, had been thoughtfully investigated by FBI agents!

The dinner was supposed to be the time when the mystery of her visit would be solved. However, everyone so thoroughly enjoyed chatting away about astronomy, teaching, the dinner, and how Grandpa had influenced Evie to become an astronomer that they decided the mystery of her visit could wait until coffee was served in a conference room after the meal. Dinner was an important time to enjoy each other's company and get to know each other. "Very serious government business can wait a bit longer," the Vice President said.

"Not too much longer," added Evie, to the smiles of the other guests.

CHAPTER 27

THE MYSTERY REVEALED

After dinner, the Vice President escorted his guests into a modern, high-tech conference room. Evie said that she hoped this was the time when the mystery would be cleared up. Just then, a photo of her favorite object, the planet Saturn, appeared on a giant, high-definition monitor. It had been taken by the robotic probe Cassini. She was well familiar with this photo and smiled when it appeared on the screen. The director of NASA began by noting that the project briefing would last an hour. In addition, there was a short briefing paper waiting for her in her room that would provide more information.

He began by asking Evie to appreciate how the amazing project she was to learn about needed a very special and rare person to be in charge of it. He told her that there was a short list of two people, and she was one of them. He explained that a similar briefing was to be held with the other candidate within a couple of days. The choice of who would direct the project would be made by the President of the United States.

She knew soon after the conversation with the Vice President began that a most important question would be put to her at the end of the briefing. That question turned out to be, "If the President offered the position to you, would you accept it?" The commitment would be to full-time leadership of a unique project for at least a decade, perhaps longer. It was a once-in-a-lifetime opportunity. However, it also meant giving up much of her current work. If she was not interested or didn't feel she was available, they would understand. Regardless of her answer or of the President's final decision, the

Vice President said that he wanted her to know the high esteem in which she was held in the scientific community, as well as in the Broxton family.

Evie blushed. Out of her sense of humility, she hardly knew what to say. She finally thanked her hosts for their confidence and pointed out that she loved a good mystery and a challenge, but that she could only answer such a question after she fully understood what was going on. The NASA director nodded in agreement and apologized for getting so excited that he'd nearly forgotten that she hadn't already been made aware of the project. After the laughter, the serious briefing got under way.

A briefing officer, Colonel Marlene Farber, began with an overview. "Saturn's sixth largest moon is called Enceladus, as you all know," he said. "It is approximately 310 miles in diameter and is covered by ice. It is a solid, rocky object rather than a gas ball like the planet Saturn itself. The latest research suggests strongly that this ice moon of Saturn is hiding an ocean of liquid water below the ice. Scientists could tell this is the case because they have observed the eruptions of 'cryo-volcanoes' spewing ice and water up from the moon's surface.

"In the name of all humanity, the nations of the world, led by the United States, would send a robot probe with the latest technology to land on the surface of Enceladus. It would drill through the ice with powerful lasers and return to Earth with samples of what is found under the ice."

Dr. Evie was fully aware of the science going on about Enceladus because she had participated in it as a major area of her professional interest at the university. She told her colleagues, "I am very pleased, not to mention excited, with the concept of this mission and curious about the technology that would be deployed. The ideas you have describe are spectacular. Project Ice-E represents great challenges to our innovation and creativity. That being said, I feel confident it could be successful, and perhaps earth shaking."

She knew the potentially great discovery that might occur: to find water on another world and bring it back to Earth for analysis. Water had been observed or theorized to exist outside of Earth, on Mars, Ganymede, and Enceladus. There was geological evidence to support this theory, including rock formations on Mars and on Earth's moon, suggesting erosion by flowing water. Mankind had not yet been able to bring back any samples. They all agreed that water was a critical ingredient for life as we know it. Further, if this moon harbored liquid water for millions of years, there was a possibility that the probe would find in the water some traces of the building blocks of life, if not life itself.

The Vice President took over the conversation and said, "The possibility of returning to Earth with a water sample is a very important part of the mission. However, there is something else as well. The 'something else' is known only to a very few people on the President's science advisory team and the national security team. Now it will be known to you."

Colonel Farber returned to the podium and continued the briefing. "There was a detection of unusual electromagnetic radiation that a top-secret air force satellite in high orbit above Earth detected. Even the academic community is not yet aware of this discovery. It happened by accident when the satellite's orbit was adjusted. The ultra-high sensitivity detection equipment on board was built and used to detect objects, such as asteroids or comets, moving in the solar system that might pose a risk of striking Earth. The satellite was focused for only a limited period of time at Enceladus by an air force intelligence officer, Major Jerry Singer, who was curious about this moon.

"Unexpected electromagnetic energy was detected coming from a particular area on the surface of Enceladus. No one knew what it was. A second intelligence reconnaissance satellite with some of the world's most advanced technology was directed to focus on the same area and confirmed the energy emissions. Within two weeks, emissions stopped. No one knew why. No one knew the source of the emissions. However, they were most unusual and exciting, especially because they displayed a regular and repeating pattern. The pattern is now being analyzed by experts at the National Security Agency. There are no results of their work to report as of yet."

The Vice President interjected. "The purpose of this project and the probe would be not only the water retrieval, as important as that is. Along with that, the probe will be designed to investigate the area from which the mysterious emissions seemed to have been coming. In fact, the nation's most advanced intelligence capabilities are being focused on this mystery. Patterns in the emissions that might suggest their nature are being studied. No explanation had yet been uncovered. Nonetheless, even if no explanation can be found, and even if the emissions did not reappear, something unusual, amazing, and unprecedented has happened. The many questions raised by the emissions have to be answered. They have to be explored!"

"Energy emissions have many possible causes," Colonel Farber continued, "such as explosions. However, emissions are also a by-product of advanced intelligence. No one knows what might be found on Enceladus, but how can we not seize the chance to send out what amounts to a digital version of the Lewis and Clark expedition to see what was out there? The possibility that there could be some form of technology, and therefore intelligence, behind the signals could be the greatest discovery in the history of humanity."

If Dr. Evie was interested in heading the project team, and if she was thereafter appointed by the President, she would lead the international effort to explore the phenomenon and find answers. Inevitably, her work would lead to more questions.

"If you become director of Project Ice-E," she was assured by the Vice President, "you would be authorized to recruit a team of top colleagues from anywhere in the world. You would have full access to all of the data from military, scientific, and intelligence resources. You would be able to draw upon the best minds in the academic, industrial, and governmental communities. In short, you would have all of the resources needed to get the job done." The Vice President added, "However, this can only happen if the necessary support and excitement and be generated for project approval. New technology would have to be created to design, launch, and guide the probe to a safe landing. You would be authorized and empowered to share news of the emissions with the rest of the world, and to create the program to keep everyone informed about what was going on. You can see how important this project is!"

"I most certainly do," Dr. Evie said emphatically. She was overwhelmed with lots of questions and possibilities. She knew that she must not speak to anyone, not even her family, about any part of the briefing or her visit to Washington, DC. She could only say that while she was in Washington, DC, she had met with leaders of the US Naval

Observatory, toured the facility, and met the staff. Until an appointment was made by the President of the United States and the possibility of the project was made public by him, it was critical that Evie honor the trust placed in her. She acknowledged the importance of a commitment to secrecy. She would tell no one anything about what she had just learned.

She promised that within a week, probably less, she would respond back with her answer. The Vice President gave her a private and secure cellular telephone number. He asked that she call him directly when she had made up her mind, or if she had any questions.

Dinner with this wonderful company of colleagues and new friends was beautiful. Evie would always remember it. Nothing could have topped the excitement of the meal better than the astounding project description she had just heard. She felt humbled and excited at the same time. She also felt nervous about what it would mean for her life and for the science she so loved.

If she became the project director, it would mean moving across the country to Washington, DC. She worried that it would mean giving up the teaching and research work that she loved for a very long time. She would either have to quit her job at the university or get an extended leave of absence. What about her salary and fringe benefits, like retirement savings and health insurance? There were many other practical, if not very personal questions, to be answered. Where would she live? Could she afford the costs of the move? She would have an awful lot to think about. The mystery of her visit had been solved, but many greater mysteries lay ahead. It would be a long few days as she thought about how she might answer. She read and reread the briefing paper before she returned it to the Secret Service as she left Blair House. She smiled to herself at the tentative name of the project. She didn't like it. She thought it was not a name that would inspire people all around the world.

She also wondered about the other candidate. Although she did not know the name of the other shortlisted scientist, she was certain that he or she would also be spending some sleepless nights in awe of what could lie ahead. Evie woke up early the next morning after her return home. She went for a long walk on the beach with her dog, Isibindi. Her mind was full of questions and worries about how her life would change if she became the project director. She couldn't discuss the offer with anyone, including Isibindi. Then she smiled, recalling that her dog's name came from the Zulu language. It meant courage—a word she had learned during her safari in South Africa. Courage was what she needed right now as she wrestled with the decision.

She tried her best to be a clear-thinking scientist and analyze the advantages and disadvantages of making such a huge change. Still, she knew this was a case where the mind of a scientist had to merge with the heart of a human being. What did her heart tell her? Of course, there were many questions about her personal life. However, they would have to be answered in due course. After all, even if she said yes to the Vice President, she might not be appointed by the President. In that case, she would soon be returning to her teaching and research work.

As she finished her walk along the beautiful shoreline, she thought she knew what she was going to say, what she must say as a scientist and as a curious human. She knew what Grandpa would advise her to say. After a good breakfast and a few final thoughts, she would be calling the Vice President!

Evie went home after her early morning walk to have her favorite quick breakfast – a blueberry muffin, some yogurt and a cup of her favorite dark Ethiopian coffee called Yirgacheffe. She made coffee every morning with her French Press coffee maker. As she started boiling the water for her coffee she thought about the phone call she would make in a few minutes. She knew that the answer to the Vice President's question would not be easy for her. It was very complicated and very important.

She imagined a great balance scale in which the many reasons to say "yes" were on one side of the balance and all the difficult complications she would face were on the other. She remembered her discussion with mom and dad when she was offered the role of the Star Princess on television. They also weighed and balanced the pluses and minuses. Then Evie got to decide. They trusted her judgment.

Now she imagined herself standing in front of that large balance scale thinking hard about what decision to make. Evie didn't want to spend years behind some desk writing memoranda to other people and attending an endless number of meetings. She was an explorer of the sky, after all.

However, she had also come to understand that being in Explorer didn't always mean being the one person who actually does all the research and all the work. It can mean being an inspiring leader. The other people on your team can share with you the thrill and the annoyances that come with exploration. As she sipped her coffee she had one more thought before finalizing the decision. It was something else that Grandpa taught her about. It was about a famous principle in science – and in life – called Occam's Razor. The idea is that when there are alternative decisions to make the best decision is most often the simplest one. Evie smiled as she remembered Grandpa helping her understand that principle to guide her decision-making.

Evie thought to herself, "I've made coffee and I've made my decision." She was sure that her family and friends would now trust her judgment again.

The call to the Vice President of the United States lasted only about ten minutes. "Mr. Vice President," Evie said, "I promised to call back with my decision about that question you were kind enough to ask me at Blair House. It would be an honor to accept an offer to lead the project if the President were to choose me. It would be incredible to serve science, my country, and my species by helping answer the great questions and solve the great mysteries involved in Project Ice-E."

"Thank you, Dr. Brown," he said. "You have started my day with wonderful news. Before the day is out I will share your answer with the President. He has already been briefed about the status of our search for the director. It probably won't be long at all before you will know his decision. Now go have a glorious day!"

Evie breathed a great sigh of relief. She had answered the greatest question ever put to her. Now it was up to the President. As for Evie, it was time for her to get to her office at the university and prepare a lecture she would give the following week. The peace of her quiet day, however, was interrupted that afternoon as her secretary knocked at the door and said rather excitedly, "Dr. Brown, you have a phone call from someone who says she is calling from the White House!"

"Dr. Brown?" asked the very professional sounding voice on the phone. "Please hold for the President of the United States." A couple of minutes later the familiar voice of the President came on the line. "Hello, Dr. Brown. I'm looking forward to meeting you after all that the Vice President has told me about you!" "Thank you, Sir," Evie responded. "It would be wonderful to meet you." "I'm hoping to get that chance, if you will accept the offer I now make to you to head Project Ice-E," said the President.

A nervous Evie blurted out her answer excitedly. Later, she laughed about it. She said, "I accept with humility and pleasure. Now, let's meet for lunch!" Fortunately, the President seemed to enjoy her answer very much. He chuckled and said, "Do you like peanut butter and jelly!" With that, the President invited her to Washington DC.to greet several members of Congress before he would introduce the new director to the nation. He added with a chuckle that this introduction would be easy since everyone already knew of the Star Princess!

Back at home after work, Evie thought quietly about her amazing day and all that was to come next. The Star Princess was ready for her new job leading a very important project! But would she be ready for the discoveries which awaited her?

EVIE'S SKY JOURNAL—A SAMPLE OF HER ASTROPHOTOS

Saturn, the amazing planet
that inspired Evie to dream.

Saturn's sixth largest moon, Enceladus,
and the source of Evie's great mystery.

The Dumbbell Nebula is a planetary nebula in the constellation of Vulpecula, the fox. It is about 1,360 light-years away. A planetary nebula is the result of gas being ejected from an exploding star. In the center of the nebula is a white dwarf star, the small remnant of the exploded star.

The beautiful Rosette Nebula is about five thousand light-years away in the constellation of Monoceros, the unicorn. It is an emission nebula. That means it consists of gases that get "excited" and glow because of the light from stars.

The Horsehead Nebula, in the constellation of Orion, is a dark nebula about 1,500 light-years away.

The Great Orion Nebula is a diffuse nebula in the constellation of Orion. Diffuse means that the nebula lacks defined boundaries. It is about 1,344 light-years away. It is a wonderful sight to see, even with a small telescope or binoculars.

The Andromeda Galaxy is the nearest to the Milky Way, although it is two and a half million light-years away. It contains about a billion stars. It is very bright and very beautiful.

Beautiful Vega is the fifth brightest star in the night sky, and it appears in the constellation Lyra, the harp. The brightest star is Sirius, the Dog Star, in the constellation of Canis Majoris. Vega is about twenty-five light-years from Earth.

The Eastern Veil Nebula is in the constellation of Cygnus, the swan. It is about 1,470 light-years from Earth. It is part of the remnant of the explosion of a giant star—a supernova.

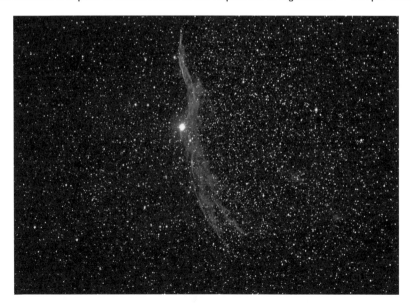

The Western Veil Nebula is part of the same supernova explosion that created the Eastern Veil Nebula. It is also about 1,470 light-years away, in the constellation of Cygnus, the swan.

The Crab Nebula is one of the most famous objects in the sky. It was first observed by Chinese astronomers in AD 1054. It is the gaseous remains of a giant star that ended its life in a massive supernova explosion. It is in the constellation of Taurus, the bull, and is about eleven thousand light-years away.

The Pleiades is a beautiful and bright open star cluster in the constellation of Taurus, the bull. It is also known as the Seven Sisters, although it contains more than one thousand stars. Its great brightness makes it visible without a telescope. It has been part of stories and folklore for thousands of years. Its stars average about 440 light-years away.

The beautiful Wild Duck open star cluster is about 6,200 light-years away from Earth in the constellation Scutum, the shield. It contains about 2,900 stars.

"Grandpa's Observatory" at his farm. Imagine Evie's excitement as she was introduced to Grandpa's huge telescopes and cameras. This is where Evie began her dream to become an explorer of the night sky.

EVIE'S AFRICA JOURNAL—A SAMPLE OF HER SAFARI PHOTOS

GRANDPA'S ADVICE FOR A LIFE OF JOY AND SUCCESS

Author's Note: Throughout this book, we follow the growth and success of the lead character, Evie. From the time she was a little girl, Evie sought and received advice from many people, particularly Mom, Dad, and Grammie. However, Grandpa was the one who inspired her most about pursuing her dreams to become an explorer of the sky. Their time together in his observatory helped her find what would be her life's passion.

Grandpa's advice to Evie goes far beyond helpful suggestions to one girl. The philosophies behind the advice are the keys to anyone's success and joy in life. The author hopes that readers will take this advice to heart, as though it was their own grandpas offering it to them. This wisdom is offered as a gift to each of you. After thinking about it, go back through *Evie, the Star Princess* and find where and how this advice was helpful in Evie's life. It can certainly be helpful in your own!

1. **Create your own army.** The friends you make throughout your life, along with colleagues at work and members of your own family, form a powerful group of people who can come to your aid if you ever need them. Sometimes members of your own army will help you in ways you may not even realize or know about. The bigger your army and the more it is filled with diverse people, the more successful you will be. In turn, you must be part of many other people's armies and stand

ready to help them. Your army makes a difference in your own life and in the lives of others.

2. **Understand the importance of respect.** No matter who you are or how famous or successful you might become, your life will be enriched by always treating people you meet with respect and kindness. Whether they are rich or poor, tall or short, healthy or ill, and no matter what their religion, race, or gender, the most successful people treat others the way they would wish to be treated.

3. **Remember that arrogance is our biggest enemy.** Arrogance is what leads to great trouble and ultimately great failure for people, as well as for communities and countries. Arrogance means excessive pride. You think you are better than someone else, but you aren't. You think your athletic team is better than every other one, but it may not be. You become a bully in the sense that you don't listen to the opinions of others, and you try to push your own thoughts and beliefs on others even if they don't want to agree with you. The Ancient Greek called excessive arrogance hubris and felt that it was this arrogance that threatened and harmed their whole civilization.

4. **Demonstrate humility in your life.** Humility is the opposite of hubris. Being humble in the way you behave toward other people means acting so that other people regard you as being willing to listen to their viewpoints. They have confidence in what you are saying. People who are humble do not brag and do not treat other people with disrespect. They are kind and caring. Humility is a behavior with which other people want to be associated.

5. **Get by with help from your friends.** People who have friends and family to be around them and spend time with them tend to be healthier and enjoy life more. You may not have a large family. In fact, you may have no brothers and sisters, and maybe even no parents. However, you can still make friends at school or at work, and by joining civic groups and service clubs in your community. Friends also include our animal friends. People who have pets, especially dogs and cats, exercise more and feel less lonely. They have another creature to cuddle with and

to share fun and sadness. Having friends as a major part of your army will make you healthier, happier, and more successful.

6. **Overcome the paralysis of inertia.** The great scientist Isaac Newton described laws of motion. His first law of motion tells us that an object will keep standing still or moving along in the same direction and speed unless some outside force moves it in a different way. The same is true of people. A person who keeps to a fixed opinion or way of acting and living will continue to do that same behavior unless some outside force affects him or her. Inertia is a form of paralysis. It is hard to move forward when you never want to move at all. It is hard to change direction if you keep moving in only one way, even when circumstances all around you change and you should be adjusting. Without change—without overcoming inertia—the full potential of your life will never be realized. We overcome inertia by being willing to try new things and adjust how we think and act as circumstances and needs change.

When we spend too many hours doing only one thing, like watching television or staring at the screens of our smart phones or tablets, we miss out on a lot of other opportunities to learn new skills and meet new people. Grandpa urges that you never fall victim to the paralysis of inertia.

7. **Become a renaissance person.** The Renaissance was a time of renewal, rebirth, and reemergence of learning, experimenting, and thinking about all the ways that things could be, rather than just how things were. It was a time when the human spirit overcame inertia and created a more exciting future for itself. You can do that in your own life. In fact, you must do that for your life to be as successful as you want it to be.

A renaissance person enjoys learning and practicing different skills. You may like science, for example, but you might also think about the arts. You may enjoy dance, drawing, or music, but you should also learn about history and nature. You may want to be at teacher in your career, but you can also take up hobbies so you can do many other things you enjoy. When you look at the totality of your life, you will see that a renaissance person with many different interests is a far more enjoyable friend to be with and to have on your team and in your life.

8. **Find thyself a teacher.** This is one of the most important keys to being successful. Always look for ways to learn from other people and take advantage of opportunities to learn. Those opportunities are all around. Sometimes they are formal teaching arrangements, such as the teachers in your school or the piano teacher your parents hire to help you learn to play. However, your teachers may also simply be those people you look at or encounter day to day—your role models. You observe how they behave or shouldn't behave. Moms and dads are people we learn most from, whether they are sitting down and formally talking to us like Grandpa did in the observatory with Evie or whether you simply watch how they behave and admire them (or wish they would behave differently). We even learn from people we don't like, such as bullies. These spoilers teach us how not to behave. We should always seek the chance to learn from others—and sometimes without them ever knowing that they are teaching us.

9. **Seek out challenges.** Challenges help us do things we might not otherwise do. If we are paralyzed by inertia, it may be a great challenge to learn how to play the violin, how to swim, or how to cook spaghetti. We may not be willing to even try! However, we miss out on great possibilities when we let inertia win. The most enjoyable life is a life full of challenges that we have learned to overcome. Challenges certainly come to each of us, whether or not we want them to. We might become ill or injured, and we have the challenge to heal and regain the strength in our arms or legs. It is not only possible but very rewarding to seek out challenges and overcome them. You may find it challenging to learn to speak Spanish or to enjoy the night sky, like Evie did. You will find your own challenges to overcome in life. When you do, you will be well on your way to becoming a renaissance person.

Don't be afraid of challenges. See them as opportunities to learn and grow. While you are there, remember that if you are nervous about some new challenge, that is the perfect time to find yourself a teacher or call out a member of your army to help you.

10. **Imagine and dream.** You can be anything you want to be—but not if you sit in front of a television set or computer screen for seven hours a day, like the average person does! You can watch less TV and spend more time imagining how it would be to do new things or use new skills.

We grow when we use our minds just as much as (and probably more than) we use our muscles. Imagination is very convenient! We can use it anytime, no matter where we are. We can travel anywhere we want to and dream about becoming anything we want to be, even in the quiet of our own room at home or when we travel. Out of that imagining and dreaming, we can plan a course of action to make our dreams come true. Evie did that. You can do the same thing!

11. **Love nature.** Respect is something that goes far beyond how we behave with other people. It also means how we find beauty and amazement in the world around us. It means going out early in the morning and watching the sunrise or watching the sunset at the end of the day. It means learning about animals, the climate, mountains, rivers, the sky, and the valleys all around us. Evie enjoyed going for walks in the meadow with her grandparents' dog. What a wonderful idea it is to go for a walk and watch nature at work. Look at the leaves, insects, and flowers. Smelling and feeling the beauty all around us, whether we live in a city or on a farm, can not only bring us a sense of amazement at the world but also give us the time and the inner peace to relax our minds. Then we can begin that imagining and dreaming process that we know is so important to our success.

12. **Develop confidence and bravery.** We overcome problems and meet challenges first by learning about what those problems and challenges are really all about. Then it is very important to take what we've learned and the advice and help we get from our friends, mixing that information with confidence in ourselves. We have to know in our hearts and minds that we can overcome obstacles. As Evie found out, it is natural to be afraid of speaking in front of large groups. If you try one of the techniques Evie learned from Grandpa—the one he describes as directed imaging—you will likely find that being afraid can be converted into being brave enough to try standing up and speaking in a group. You may find that it was not so

difficult a problem as you'd thought. A bit of bravery and confidence is available to all of us and can help in everything we do.

13. **Have a sense of humor and a sense of fun.** Being serious all the time is very unfortunate and does not make you the kind of person who other people want to be around. A speaker named Michael Josephson once said, "Some people brighten a room when they enter it; others, when they leave!" If you have humor and a positive attitude, it will be contagious. Other people will think of you as someone they want to listen to and want to follow.

14. **Don't postpone joy.** Find things that you really enjoy doing. Find hobbies you enjoy and charities you want to support. Then figure out how to get involved with them. Evie enjoyed knitting and music. These hobbies helped her relax even though she faced many pressures. Our lives are full of opportunities to do things and see things that make us smile and make us happy. We should not waste those opportunities. Figure out how to add a strong dose of joy into your life every day!

15. **Act now to put off the day when something bad happens.** This is very important advice from Grandpa that can profoundly help everyone. It is advice to prevent very serious troubles from entering our lives. Grandpa meant that we should look at the risks we face in life and take action right away—not later but now—to reduce those risks. Many of these actions are very simple. For example, put on a seat belt every time you get into a car. That can prevent all sorts of very bad trouble if there is an auto accident. Drinking and smoking are things we know are not healthy. We shouldn't hurt ourselves by doing them.

There are some risks that we cannot totally control. There may be a giant hurricane coming, or you may live in a place where there might be earthquakes. Even then, however, we can develop ways to reduce the harm that might come along with these monsters. We might store some extra water or food. We might have a plan to leave an area when a hurricane is coming. We may talk with friends about spending times of danger with one another. There is much that we can do, even when the risks are tremendous.

We are reminded by Grandpa that when we know a danger is out there and we do nothing, we are falling victim to the great danger of inertia. We could have done something, but we were too lazy to move off the couch. We thought we were too busy to act to reduce the risks. Now we know, after the problem has struck and harmed us, that we could have and should have taken action. Grandpa called this very important bit of advice "Not walking by something wrong." When you see something wrong, when you see someone who needs help, or when you see some way to improve something important, go ahead and act to turn that something wrong into something made better because of what you did.

16. **Act with compelling urgency.** This is related to several other key philosophies. When you decide that you would love to learn something new, go for it and do it! Don't make excuses. Don't promise to do it next week or next year—do it now! Act with urgency! The same is true when you see something wrong. Don't ignore it, because it will probably get worse. Don't put up with the bad behavior of the bully. Instead, act to improve or correct the problem right away. Substitute urgency for inertia, and your life will be better.

17. **Say thanks.** When something wonderful happens to you or to someone else, take the time to thank the person who cared enough to do that wonderful thing. There are many ways to say thanks. People enjoy being thanked, and it encourages even more wonderful behavior. We don't say thanks enough in the world, but you can make a difference and change that.

You can surprise someone by doing a kind thing as a way to thank him or her. In turn, that person will thank you. Bring a flower to your teacher or to someone with whom you work. Take your mom or dad out for ice cream, or do something nice they don't expect. Maybe you can wash the car for them, take out the trash, or write them a note of thanks. A gesture like holding a door open for someone, or thanking veterans, firefighters, or police officers for their service, may seem like a small thing. But such things are often remembered for a very long time. Your kindness defines the kind of person you are for others.

If you follow Grandpa's advice, you will get to look back at a life of joy and success. Certainly, we will all have times of sadness and problems in our lives. Some will be huge, but most will be very small. Grandpa's advice can help you with all of these problems. His advice can help you look back many, many years later at how wonderful your life has been and will continue to be, not only for you and your family but for other people who may never have met you in person.

Now, how about going back through *Evie, the Star Princess* and looking for examples of how Evie applies the lessons learned from Grandpa? Imagine how you too can apply those lessons in your own life. Finally, don't simply think about examples of others using Grandpa's advice—get on with doing it yourself. See how much better things will be for you!

Thank you for reading about Evie's adventures. She and I hope you will create many rewarding adventures for yourself!

Printed in the United States
By Bookmasters